Clair-de-Lune

Clair-de-Lune

By Cassandra Golds

Alfred A. Knopf  New York

THIS IS A BORZOI BOOK PUBLISHED BY ALFRED A. KNOPF

Copyright © 2006 by Cassandra Golds

Jacket illustration copyright © 2006 by Sonia Kretschmar

Interior spot illustrations © 2006 by Sophie Blackall

Published in the United States by Alfred A. Knopf, an imprint of Random House Children's Books,
a division of Random House, Inc., New York, and simultaneously in Canada
by Random House of Canada Limited, Toronto.

Distributed by Random House, Inc., New York.

Originally published in Australia by Penguin Books Australia in 2004.

"A Mouse Lullaby" was first published by the NSW Department of Education
and Training's *School Magazine Blast Off #8*, September 2000.

KNOPF, BORZOI BOOKS, and the colophon are registered trademarks of Random House, Inc.

www.randomhouse.com/kids

Library of Congress Cataloging-in-Publication Data

Golds, Cassandra.
Clair-de-Lune / Cassandra Golds. — 1st American ed.
p. cm.
SUMMARY: A talking mouse takes a talented young ballet dancer to an enchanted
world where she explores, with the help of a kind monk, why she cannot speak.
ISBN 0-375-83395-1 (trade) — ISBN 0-375-93395-6 (lib. bdg.)
[1. Ballet dancing—Fiction. 2. Mutism, Elective—Fiction.
3. Emotional problems—Fiction. 4. Mice—Fiction.] I. Title.
PZ7.G5699CI 2006
[Fic]—dc22   2005016771

Printed in the United States of America
10 9 8 7 6 5 4 3 2 1
First American Edition

For Jonathan Shaw

Clair-de-Lune

The Girl Who Could Not Speak

Once upon a time—one hundred years ago, and half as many years again—there lived a girl called Clair-de-Lune, who could not speak.

She lived with her grandmother in an attic at the top of a very tall, very narrow, very old building, with six floors and twelve rickety flights of stairs climbing up and down precariously between them. They were very poor. But they were also very *gentilles*, which means that Clair-de-Lune's grandmother thought a good deal about table manners and ladylike behavior, and would rather starve than be considered ill-mannered. In winter, the attic was cold, and the wind blew through the cracks around the windowpanes, and snow floated in through the ceiling. But in spring and summer, the sparrows and the swallows and the doves and the pigeons flew in flocks past the attic windows, and Clair-de-Lune would wake in the morning to the strange, lovely sound of their wings beating against their breasts.

Clair-de-Lune's grandmother had been a ballerina, and so had Clair-de-Lune's mother. So it will not surprise you when I say that Clair-de-Lune spent every morning, Monday to Saturday, in a large, long room three floors below with four and twenty other girls and boys and a strict ballet master by the name of Monsieur Dupoint, for she was learning to be a dancer, too. In the afternoons she studied geography and history and French and Italian and went to the market for her grandmother, who was very frail (although as slim and straight-backed as a young tree) and rarely moved from the attic. On Sundays, Clair-de-Lune went to church, where she opened her mouth in time with the music but did not sing.

Why was it that Clair-de-Lune could not speak? Ah! Nobody knew. But Clair-de-Lune's mother had died when she was a baby, and it was thought to have something to do with that.

Clair-de-Lune's mother—who had been known as *La Lune*, which means "the moon"—had been much celebrated for a famous *pas seul* that came at the end of a tragic and beautiful ballet about swans, who, it is said, are mute until the very last moments of their lives, when they give forth the loveliest of all songs. Many years before the first performance of *Swan Lake*, and many years more before Anna Pavlova conquered the world with *The Dying Swan*, La Lune danced the role of a swan mortally wounded by the crossbow of a hunter, in a long white *tutu* made of layers and layers of tulle and swans' feathers. And though La Lune made no sound, for dancers do not, there was one night when all the audience swore that she was singing the most unearthly song, as if her dancing was so beautiful that you could hear it. On that night, when she sank to the boards at the end of her *pas seul*, folding herself like a bird, she rested her head among the tulle and the feathers of her skirt, and did not rise again.

"*Brava! Brava!*" came the shouts from the audience, whose clapping and cheering were like thunder. At first, no one understood that anything was wrong. It was some moments before the audience, at first uncertain, grew quiet; before the curtains were drawn hurriedly and a doctor called; before the audience began to whisper, then to murmur among themselves. Then came the announcement, with the head of the Company in tears: "Ladies and gentlemen, La Lune is dead! The doctor says her heart was weak—too weak for her to dance. If only we had known . . . !" and the sobs of the audience, and the flowers, which poured in from all over the country for weeks.

Some who were backstage on the night La Lune died said it was not singing they heard, but speech—that La Lune, the mute swan, the ballerina, had died trying to say something.

As for Clair-de-Lune—well, La Lune's public did not even know she existed. But she, too, was backstage that night, and though she was only a tiny baby, she must have understood something. For, from that day to this, she had never uttered a word.

Did Clair-de-Lune mind about not speaking? Ah, reader! It seemed to her that as each day passed, the weight of things unsaid grew heavier and heavier on her heart.

Clair-de-Lune Cries as if Her Heart Would Break

Every morning, come rain or sunshine—even in winter, when the snow lay on the ground—Clair-de-Lune would kneel on the window seat, push open the casement, lean her elbows on the windowsill, and gaze out of the attic, trying to speak.

Sometimes, when the sun was shining, or even in the gentle rain, she would feel happy while she was doing this, because there was a kind of peace in looking out the window, a kind of privacy. Suddenly she was alone with the view, and the view almost seemed to look back at her, liking her, and not minding that she was mute.

But most often she was sad, because she longed to be able to speak, and yet, no matter how much she longed, no matter how hard she tried, no words came. She would sit gazing out at the acres and acres of brownish red rooftops, for that was all that could be seen from the attic window—brownish red slate

4

roofs, sloping unevenly; drainpipes; a steeple in the distance; a black cat picking its way over the roof opposite; chimneys; pigeons; sparrows; swallows; doves; and on sunny days a small blue square, which was the sky. And as she gazed, she would be overwhelmed by longing, until the tears pricked at her eyes and overflowed and the red roofs swam together.

And then her grandmother would call to her to hurry up and finish dressing, for she must be at her class by nine o'clock, and she would pull in her head and obey.

To class every morning, Clair-de-Lune wore rose-pink stockings and practice shoes and a sharply waisted white muslin practice dress with matching pantalettes, which extended three inches below the hem of her calf-length skirt. A black sash went around her waist. The dress was *décolletée*—that is, it left her throat and shoulders bare—and, like all the other girls, she parted her hair in the middle and smoothed it back modestly into a chignon that rested on the nape of her neck. A black snood kept her hair in check. The whole ensemble was a compromise between modesty and the very real practical need to see as much as possible of what the limbs and body were doing during a ballet class. Modesty had prevailed, however. Clair-de-Lune was learning to dance *en pointe*, and she carried her *pointe* shoes with her to class in a threadbare little reticule, together with a clean handkerchief. She had blocked the shoes herself, as dancers did in those days, with extra stitching and starched muslin wrapped around her toes. When it was cold she wore her mother's warm woolen *pelisse* to and from class. Fortunately, because the school was held in the same building three floors below, she need not go outside.

Breakfast each morning was the same: bread, a scrape of chocolate, and milk coffee heated in a saucepan on their little potbellied stove. There was never quite enough to eat, and not surprisingly, Clair-de-Lune and her grandmother were both very thin.

"Sit up straight, child," Clair-de-Lune's grandmother would say. "Remember, your back should not touch the chair."

And then it would be time to leave.

Every morning, Clair-de-Lune would make her way down six flights of steps—two for each floor—and wonder, as she passed each doorway, what lay behind it. On the fourth floor there lived an opera singer—a baritone—and often, although not early in the morning, Clair-de-Lune would hear him singing his scales, or practicing an aria. The building had many actors and dancers and singers and artists living in it, but it was large and complicated and Clair-de-Lune knew that many of its people, and much of its comings and goings, were a mystery to her.

Just how much of a mystery she was yet to find out.

All the way down the last four flights of steps, more and more clearly as she approached, Clair-de-Lune could hear the ballet school's pianist warming up. (He wore gray woolen gloves with the fingers snipped off them as he played, because his hands were always cold.) Depending on the season, and if the day was going to be a sunny one, there would be warm, bright patches of sunlight in the dusty windows of the landings between the stairways. In one of these, arranged gracefully with an eye to the possibility of passing portrait painters (or so it seemed), Clair-de-Lune would often encounter elderly Mrs.

Costello's Minette, who would purr with immediate rapture when stroked, shutting her green eyes with a sort of regal gratitude. Then, as Clair-de-Lune rounded the corner and began to descend the last flight, she would come upon the large double doorway with the stern sign on the wall beside it:

**MONSIEUR DUPOINT'S SELECT
DANCING ACADEMY
FOR THE CHILDREN OF ARTISTES
WHO ASPIRE TO ENTER
THEIR PARENTS' PROFESSION**

Girls and boys milled around it as they arrived for the morning— girls in rose-pink stockings and white practice frocks, boys in calf-length black breeches, black belts, and short white muslin vests—and always, at this point, Clair-de-Lune's heart would quail, and sometimes it was all she could do to keep her feet going in the school's direction, so strongly did they seem to want her to turn and retreat back up the stairs. But on she would go, just a little more slowly at first, and then quickly, as she ducked her head and squeezed past them through the doorway.

"Snob," one of the girls—usually Milly Twinkenham, who had bright red hair and nut-brown eyes—would murmur. "Won't talk, just because her mother was La Lune. . . ."

For in all the class, Clair-de-Lune had not one friend.

But inside, it was easier.

Clair-de-Lune did not like to arrive early, while everyone was still chatting, for of course she was unable to explain why she could not. She always tried to reach the door just at the moment Monsieur Dupoint called his class to order—from which point there was always complete, disciplined silence. Then, quiet like the others, she would scuttle to the *barre* and wait, in first position, for Monsieur Dupoint to begin the class.

"*Attention, s'il vous plaît, mesdemoiselles, messieurs,*" he would say. "We shall commence, of course, with *pliés!* First position. Draw yourselves up. Tails tucked under. Tummies pulled in. Heads erect. *And—*"

Monsieur Dupoint was a thin, small man who seemed to live on medicinal tea, which steamed in his cup throughout his classes and filled the room with a faint herbal scent. He often behaved as if he were teaching through a splitting headache, as if everything was too much for him and the world a dreadful place—but as the class wore on he would become more and more cheerful, a little grudgingly at first, and then as if he had forgotten what he was annoyed about. He tried not to show it, but in fact he had a very soft spot for Clair-de-Lune, as he had danced with her mother and every day would see a little movement or an attitude of the head or arms that reminded him of her. He often stole secret, proud glances in her direction, for he felt convinced that one day she would be a great dancer like her mother and grandmother, and he would be remembered as her teacher.

And indeed, Clair-de-Lune loved to dance. She loved the long, dusty wooden room, its walls covered in mirrors; she loved the sight of the long *barre* suspended along the sides, and the feel of it in her hands. She loved the strict, precise sound of Monsieur Dupoint's voice as he counted time or stopped the music to scold them and then to demonstrate, exquisitely, how something should be done. She loved to move, to work, until her limbs were warm and supple and her face glowing. But most of all, Clair-de-Lune loved dancing because it was a way to speak, even if she could not do so with her lips and her tongue and her mouth. When she was dancing, her arms and legs spoke, and her hands and feet spoke, and her body and the carriage of her head spoke, too. And she felt that just a little of the weight on her heart, the weight of things unsaid, would be lifted.

Ah, but what is dance without music? If it were possible, Clair-de-Lune loved music even more than dance—for she knew that without it, none of these other things could have happened.

The school's pianist was a poor young music student with a thin, haggard face and dark eyes. He played patiently through all the exercises, keeping strict time and stopping and starting whenever Monsieur Dupoint required. But at the end of each morning's class, he would play beautiful music just for the love of it as everyone collected their things, said goodbye, and left; and Clair-de-Lune would linger, unnoticed, in order to hear it to the end.

On one particular morning as the class ended, when each girl had made her *révérence* and each boy his *salut* and Monsieur Dupoint had dismissed them, young Mr. Sparrow, the pianist, began to play the most beautiful music Clair-de-Lune had ever heard.

And because of this, something happened.

In fact, because of this, many things happened.

At first, so that she could listen, she sat on the floor, pretending to fuss with the ribbons that tied up her shoes, crossing and recrossing them. But soon she forgot to pretend to do anything. As Mr. Sparrow continued to play, more and more beautifully, she slowly let go of the ribbons, sat forward, rose to her feet . . . then crept across the room to the piano.

For it seemed to Clair-de-Lune that the music was filled with longing—a longing so gentle, and yet so intense, that it would break her heart. It seemed to be asking something from her that she, in turn, longed to give. And yet she didn't know what it was, or how to give it.

When at last Mr. Sparrow finished playing, Clair-de-Lune's heart was so full that for a moment she thought that a spell had been broken, and that when she opened her mouth she would be able to say something. Tears filled her eyes; they overflowed and ran down her cheeks. She stood there at the piano, leaning forward slightly in her eagerness, and took a breath as if to speak.

But Mr. Sparrow was sitting, silent and still, staring at the piano, lost in his own sadness. After a moment, without even noticing her, he closed it gently. Then he got up, collected his coat from the peg, and, hands in pockets, shoulders slumped, made his dejected way down the room and out through the door.

For a moment, in the long, dusty wooden room, there was complete silence.

Clair-de-Lune stood frozen at the piano. She had wanted

to thank him, to ask him what the music was. He had been sad; he had not known that anyone was listening.

She had wanted, so much, just to tell him that she was there. . . .

The room was empty. Everyone had gone. Clair-de-Lune crept into a dusty corner behind the piano, folded herself into her white practice dress, and began—silently—to sob as if her heart would break.

But nothing in this world is utterly silent, not even a girl who cannot speak. Clair-de-Lune's crying was not silent, but so soft that only a mouse could have heard it.

A Girl Who Cannot Speak Meets a Mouse Who Can

Now, in the back corner of the large, long, dusty room in which the ballet school held its classes, there was a mouse hole. And if any cat had looked inside it, she would have been very surprised by what she saw.

For the mouse hole was a tiny replica of the room outside it. Along its walls were mouse-sized mirrors, put together painstakingly from discarded powder compacts. Suspended halfway down along both sides there was a mouse-sized *barre*, constructed from toothpicks. Standing beside it, in first position, was a mouse-sized mouse.

As the music finished, he performed a gracious *salut* to himself in the mirror. Then, with the neat, disciplined, supple movements of all dancers, he skipped across to a tiny chair in the corner of his mouse hole, on which he kept a worn towel. He dried the perspiration from his fur, folded the towel neatly, draped it over the back of the chair, and pulled on his coat and scarf so that his muscles would not get cold and stiff and he would not catch a chill. He was just about to set off for lunch when he heard the sound of crying.

The dancer mouse poked his nose carefully out into the air of the room outside. His whiskers twitched. You couldn't be too careful. There was a Cat living in the building, after all.

He saw Clair-de-Lune immediately. His hearing had told him where she was even before he looked.

He hesitated, his ears twitching with wonder.

Then, timidly, running along the skirting boards in fits and starts, he approached her. He stopped approximately six inches from the hem of her skirt; it was all he needed, he knew, for a running start in case she proved to be unfriendly.

Now, normally, he would not have ventured to talk to a human—animals rarely do. And people didn't always like mice, he knew.

But of all the students—and he had been watching each of them most carefully for many weeks—she was his favorite. She was the most careful, the most disciplined, the most serious of all the dancers. She understood.

The mouse loved dancing more than anything else in the world. It made him very happy. He could not understand how anyone who danced as beautifully as Clair-de-Lune could be so sad.

Life, for mice, is very simple.

He cleared his throat.

"Mademoiselle," he said gently, "excuse me, but why do you weep?"

Clair-de-Lune stopped crying at once.

For a moment, she was perfectly still.

Then, slowly, she lifted her head.

She stared at him mutely.

The mouse rolled his eyes and slapped his forehead with his little paw. "Ah! Pardon me, I beg you. How could I be so clumsy, so—so—clodhopping? Allow me, please, to introduce myself. My name is Bonaventure. It means 'happy chance' or 'good fortune'! It is a name that lifts the spirits and lightens the heart, even if I do say so myself. Ah, but living up to it— there's the rub! I am, as you can see, a mouse—but a dancer mouse . . . It is easy to forget to introduce yourself to someone you feel you know well—I have watched you dance many times, mademoiselle. I admire your work very much—and I think Monsieur Dupoint does, too!"

Clair-de-Lune blinked, and swallowed, and inclined her head in a kind of dazed politeness.

"Would you like me to sing you a lullaby?" offered the mouse kindly. "My mother used to sing beautiful lullabies. It is little known that mice sing some of the loveliest lullabies in the world. . . . All of ours were about the sea. I grew up by the sea, you see, in a fisherman's cottage. My cradle—which I shared with my nine brothers and sisters—was a seashell. Imagine that! I have only to smell fish—and you do smell fish around here, have you ever noticed? The elderly lady in number twelve keeps a cat, you know—just a whiff of fish, as I say, or the nibble of an oyster, and it all comes back to me. But when I grew up I wanted to see the world! Become an *artiste*! So I jumped on a cart and ended up here. . . ."

He paused, considering her.

"What is wrong?" he asked again, gently, as she stared at him hopelessly. "Don't you know?"

Suddenly his whiskers twitched.

"You don't know about this house, do you? Nothing can go wrong here, you know. Not really. Not forever. No matter how bad it seems."

Clair-de-Lune gazed at him in wonder.

"I know what I'll do!" he said, making up his mind all at once. "I shall introduce you to my friend Brother Inchmahome. There is a monastery not far from here, you know! He lives in it. He is interested in everyone and everything. Moreover, his heart was once broken, therefore he is very wise. He will know what to do. No problem is too large for him! 'Brother Inchmahome,' I said to him when I first arrived, 'I am an *artiste*. I was born to dance. My love for the dance is such that my very heart aches whenever I think of it. But I am a mouse. Is it not foolish for a mouse to wish to dance?'

"My dear old mother thought so, you know," the mouse added, leaning toward Clair-de-Lune in a confidential manner. "She thought it important to accept one's Limitations. Ah, but I said to myself, is that a life?

" 'Mice are the best dancers,' Brother Inchmahome said to me. 'One has only to see a mouse move to know that. Mice dance with their whiskers. They dance with their tails. They spend their lives dancing. It is they who taught us. . . . How can it be absurd for a mouse to dance?'

"So you see, I plan to establish my own school, with a view

to ultimately starting a company. Can you imagine it—the exquisiteness of a troupe of mice, dancing? One day, little mademoiselle, one day . . ."

But just at that moment, they heard a voice out on the landing.

"Scat!" they heard faintly, and then, "Wretched creature!"

Then the large wooden double doors opened with a resounding bang and Monsieur Dupoint reentered the room. Clair-de-Lune was so startled she leaped guiltily to her feet. But Bonaventure was used to danger. "Tomorrow morning, early, mademoiselle, I will visit you," he called gaily as he skipped across the floor to the skirting boards. "And then I will take you to the monastery . . . ," she thought she heard him say as, out of the corner of her eye, she glimpsed his tiny gray form receding down the room. Monsieur Dupoint advanced toward her from the opposite direction, carrying two hot bread rolls in a white handkerchief, which he had bought from the baker downstairs. Even in her confusion, Clair-de-Lune was surprised to find that he did not live entirely on herbal tea after all.

"Ah, Clair-de-Lune, still here?" he said kindly, seeing neither the mouse nor his pupil's guilty expression. "What are you doing here *toute seule*—all alone? Back to your grandmother, child—she will be wondering where you are. And give her my very kindest regards. Tell her I will be paying her a visit sometime soon!"

Clair-de-Lune curtsied, then scuttled across the room and out the door. Just as she passed through it, she thought she saw, again out of the corner of her eye, a small gray form disappearing into a hole in the skirting board.

"And mind you don't let that infernal cat in," Monsieur Dupoint called after her. "The *pas de chat*," he added—his usual little joke—"is the only cat allowed in this school."

The door clattered behind her.

I must get that fixed, thought Monsieur Dupoint, and he set the kettle on the little potbellied stove that stood at the top of the room, thinking to make himself a soothing *tisane* to drink with his rolls. He gazed out the deep window at the red roofs and drainpipes and pigeons. Directly opposite was the back of the theater where the Company performed every night. And the Company was a hundred years old this spring. What a tradition!

Monsieur Dupoint thought fondly of Clair-de-Lune, and sighed as he considered what he thought of as her affliction.

Ah, he thought, *but the child can dance. Why should she need to speak?*

We Meet Madame Nuit

Up in the attic room, three floors above, Clair-de-Lune's grandmother, Madame Nuit, was indeed awaiting her return. But she had not noticed that Clair-de-Lune was late. While Clair-de-Lune was at class, she had dusted, as usual, and swept, washed up the breakfast things, aired the linen, and made the beds. And she had prepared Clair-de-Lune's meager lunch— bread and a sliver of cheese. Now she sat straight-backed in her chair, her black lace shawl draped over her shoulders, reading a stern book about discipline and self-denial and the vital importance of single-mindedness in one's devotion to one's art. But she could not give her mind to it. Instead, she found herself thinking of Clair-de-Lune's mother, for today was the anniversary of La Lune's death.

La Lune had been a great dancer, there was no denying it. But she had been a wild girl, whose wild hair had given Clair-de-Lune's grandmother endless trouble. No matter how many pins, no matter how much lacquer, no matter how tightly twisted or firmly braided, still its black curls would escape in tendrils around her face and neck during performances, distracting the audience, Clair-de-Lune's grandmother felt, from the perfection of her dancing.

Clair-de-Lune's hair, on the other hand, her grandmother reflected with satisfaction, was as fair as moonlight, as soft as down, and straight, but not too straight—entirely biddable.

La Lune had been just as bad as her hair. A wild girl who would not be content with dancing, who had to go off chasing after disreputable young men! Well, one disreputable young man, anyway. The love letters—intercepted! The tears and scenes! The ingratitude!

Clair-de-Lune's grandmother sat still as stone in her chair. Her beautiful face—so stern and austere—was like the face of a statue. She knew that her daughter had died of a broken heart, and she had never forgiven her for it.

She did not see Clair-de-Lune's inability to speak as an affliction. She saw it as a gift, a blessing. Why should the child need to speak? She could dance, couldn't she? And speaking—Clair-de-Lune's grandmother shifted in her seat with irritation—speaking led to friends, and friends to young men, and young men to lovers, and lovers . . . ah! to disappointment and ruin!

For it seemed to Clair-de-Lune's grandmother that all of life—apart from The Dance—turned to dust in one's mouth. Life was like a rose that crumbled in one's hand when one reached out to take it, or a shining golden fruit that was bitter when bitten into. But The Dance—ah, The Dance! Now *there* was something that did not disappoint! There was something whose beauty did not fade! There, indeed, was a life. And there was no life outside it that Clair-de-Lune's grandmother could see.

She closed her book and laid it on the table, then got up restlessly and went to the window. She had lived almost all her life in this city, among *émigrés* like herself, and yet she still felt a stranger in a strange land. She had been born in the year of the Revolution; her parents, both dancers, had fled with her before she had smiled her first smile. But the only country she really belonged in was the Country of The Dance.

She stared out the window. Like Monsieur Dupoint, she also could see from her window the back of the theater where the ballet performed every night. Inside that building, on this day, nearly as long ago as the span of Clair-de-Lune's life, her daughter had died.

There was nothing wrong with the child, she thought again. Indeed, she was a model granddaughter. Quiet. Obedient. Disciplined. And she had the makings of a great—a truly great—dancer. All was as it should be. Well, as good as it could be in this sad world.

But as she stood at the window, gazing unseeing at the back of the theater opposite, she found her mind returning to a day many years ago, the day after that terrible last night at the theater—the night her daughter had died.

It had been dark inside the room, glowing with the dim light of fire and candles, and heavy with a scent she did not recognize. She had come with the baby through wind and rain; she had wrapped the child well, but her little face was cold and damp and she was crying weakly (as if she knew).

"The fee," said the woman.

Clair-de-Lune's grandmother was startled.

"The fee," the woman repeated. "Once you have paid me, I must answer all your questions with perfect truth. Until you have paid me, I may not speak."

Clair-de-Lune's grandmother drew out a purse full of coins and placed it on the table between them. The fee was hefty—more than she could afford. But this woman had been advising the very highest in the land! And what was the point of going to someone you were not sure of?

The woman looked down at the baby and laid her hand on its cheek. Instantly the baby stopped crying and looked up fixedly at the stranger. It was almost as if the child were speaking to her, without words.

"She has it in her to become a great dancer," the woman pronounced.

"Like her mother!" breathed Clair-de-Lune's grandmother.

"Only one thing has the power to stop her."

"What? What?"

And the woman leaned over and whispered in Clair-de-Lune's grandmother's ear.

Clair-de-Lune's grandmother sat back in horror.

Just like her mother, she breathed.

"Ah, but you do not understand!" said the woman earnestly. She was frightened by something she saw in Clair-de-Lune's grandmother's face. "Yes, it has the power to stop her—but she cannot have one without the other. If she tries to do either one on its own, she will starve!"

But Clair-de-Lune's grandmother would not—could not—listen.

"What can I do? How can I stop it?"

"Stop it? But you must not stop it!"

"I will—I must—if I can. Can I?"

The woman's face was stricken. And yet, under the fortune-tellers' law, she was bound to tell anything she was asked.

"Take the bird," she said at length, reluctantly. "Cage it. That will stop it."

Clair-de-Lune's grandmother knew what she meant. For when a child sleeps, a little magic bird flies out of the child's heart and roosts nearby, sometimes on the bedpost, sometimes on the windowsill, sometimes—who knows where?—breathing in and out swiftly and murmuring to itself. When the child wakes, the bird returns, flying into her heart the very moment before she opens her eyes.

That night, while Clair-de-Lune slept, her grandmother crept into her room and tempted the bird onto her finger with a piece of candied quince. Then she put it in a golden cage she had purchased especially for the purpose. The bird's heart, which was visible through the silver feathers of its breast, glowed red and gold. The baby Clair-de-Lune laughed and clapped her hands the next morning to see the pretty bird in its golden cage. But one day soon after, somehow, the cage door was left open and the bird escaped, through the little door and out the window.

Neither of them had ever seen it again.

Deep in her heart, Clair-de-Lune's grandmother knew that that was why Clair-de-Lune could not speak, and it worried her that the bird was not where it should be—in the cage.

When Clair-de-Lune's grandmother left, the fortune-teller wept for having been forced to tell her what she did. But then she drew close to her crystal ball, whispered words to it and caressed it, and finally leaned over it attentively. A tear fell on the glass, and as she watched the scenes it showed her, the fortune-teller smiled faintly with satisfaction.

"All will be well," she murmured.

Duty, Discipline, and Devotion to The Dance

Anyone who really knew Clair-de-Lune could have seen, the moment she came in the door, that she had a secret. But her grandmother did not see.

She does not know when I am happy, thought Clair-de-Lune. *She does not know when I am sad. And yet it still seems to me that she knows everything.*

Clair-de-Lune had not wasted any time wondering at the fact that Bonaventure, a mouse, could talk. Neither had she wasted any time wondering that, apparently, he could dance as well. Nothing seemed surprising in this strange world. What she had spent some time doing was worrying—for although it was not clear to her exactly why, she felt quite sure that her grandmother would not approve of her talking to mice. And if her grandmother disapproved of talking to mice, Clair-de-Lune was quite certain it must be wrong.

"Ah, there you are, child. Change your frock quickly. Then come to luncheon!"

Clair-de-Lune changed swiftly into her dove-gray and white striped day gown with its pink sash and white collar, and sat meekly at the table. Then (as usual) she ate, as daintily as she could, while (as usual) her grandmother watched her like a cat watches a mouse.

"Straighten your back, child. How many times must I tell you? It should not touch the chair. And where are your feet?"

Clair-de-Lune uncurled them from around the chair legs and placed them dutifully on the floor.

Of course, she had not spoken to the mouse. Not a single word! Clair-de-Lune almost smiled. Almost. For she knew that listening to him alone was quite criminal enough—and as for going with him to visit a monastery!

What monastery could he be talking about?

"Don't dawdle over your meal, child. How will we get through your lessons at this rate? There are errands to run as well, remember. You must try not to be such a slow eater!"

Clair-de-Lune *was* a slow eater. She did not do it deliberately and was not even aware of why she did it—but there was a reason. The truth was that eating slowly made her feel as if she was eating more. She was always hungry, but was so used to it that she could hardly tell anymore.

They had not always been so poor. In the days of La Lune's celebrity, they had been almost rich. They had lived in a beautiful little house opposite the park and had had a cook called Mrs. Mobbs and a maid called Nellie and a little King Charles spaniel called Chouchou and plenty to eat. But although Clair-de-Lune's grandmother had economized ferociously after La Lune died, the money had soon begun to run out. Now—and until Clair-de-Lune could begin to earn something as a grown-up dancer—they were living on the charity of the Company.

Clair-de-Lune's lessons were invented by her grandmother, and their purpose was to keep her sensible. So, for two hours every day, Clair-de-Lune studied the most sensible subjects her grandmother could think of. She pored over the huge old atlas and learned by heart, from north to south, the coastal towns of exotic countries (geography). She memorized long lists of kings, queens, dates, wars, shipwrecks, public executions, and natural disasters (history). As her grandmother had a ballerina's knowledge of French and a musician's knowledge of Italian, Clair-de-Lune studied both of these (languages—vocational). She mended her clothes (domestic economy). She added and subtracted, multiplied and divided (learning to live within one's income). And (her favorite) she read Improving Literature (discipline—self).

But she read no stories of friendship or love—her grandmother made sure of that.

Clair-de-Lune's reading was restricted to stories of Duty, Discipline, and Devotion to Higher Causes—and it must be said that Clair-de-Lune found many of these quite thrilling. Of course, finding Improving Literature that was entirely suitable for Clair-de-Lune's grandmother's purposes was a constant problem. Even the Bible had to be censored, and although she sent Clair-de-Lune to church because she thought of it as a Steadying Influence, she was always a little worried the child would hear something subversive there.

But Clair-de-Lune also read stories of the great dancers—of their Discipline and Devotion to The Dance—and these she loved best of all. In a series of volumes entitled *Artists and Their Sacrifices*—dainty little lavender-scented books with white kid covers and yellowing, gilt-edged pages—she read of Sergei Superblatov, who had danced through an entire ballet with a broken leg without anyone even suspecting, enduring excruciating pain and throwing away the rest of his life as a dancer rather than disrupt the performance; of Lisette L'Oiseau, who had refused to visit the love of her life on his deathbed because it would mean missing half a day's rehearsal; of Eleanor Wood, who never ate at all because she believed that food made her heavy on her feet and who, one day, during a particularly magnificent leap, had simply floated away like a dandelion seed, never to be seen again.

Most thrilling of all, on special occasions—and today was one of those—Clair-de-Lune's grandmother would allow Clair-de-Lune to climb up on a chair and reach to the top cupboard, where a large scrapbook was kept, filled with press clippings from La Lune's glittering career. Clair-de-Lune would bring it carefully down to the table and leaf through it as her heart thumped with excitement and almost broke when she came, every time, once again, so suddenly, to the terrible clipping that announced her mother's death.

"LA LUNE DIES ONSTAGE"

said the headline, and Clair-de-Lune's grandmother would talk sternly about La Lune's bravery and nobility in giving up her life for The Dance; of how she had died, literally, with her *pointe* shoes on. She always talked of La Lune as if she belonged among the pages of *Artists and Their Sacrifices*, as if she had been nothing more complicated, nothing more human than a Perfect Dancer, who had thought about and loved and done nothing other than dance, and who had not so much died as ascended to take her place among the exalted company of good examples. She never told Clair-de-Lune about what sort of stories her mother liked, or what her first words had been, about whether she preferred cats to dogs, or what her favorite song was. She never told Clair-de-Lune that her mother had been Wild. She never told the girl that her mother had died of a broken heart.

But when Clair-de-Lune thought about her mother, as she did very often, it was those things she wondered about—the day-to-day things, the human things. Of course, she never forgot her mother's stature as a dancer: it was a constant, exhausting ideal, ever present, and yet impossible to live up to. But although this sense of her mother as one whom she must strive to emulate quite dominated her young life, it was her wonderings about her as a person that interested Clair-de-Lune most.

What had she laughed at? What had she cried about? How often had she caught cold? Had she ever felt too tired to go on?

Sometimes, when she was daydreaming in this way, something strange would happen.

She would begin to feel frightened.

It was almost as if someone, or something, deep inside Clair-de-Lune was trying to talk to her, from behind many lay-

28

ers of—what? She did not know. But whatever this stuff was, the layers upon layers of it muffled the voice so pitilessly that the sound of it was terrifying.

So Clair-de-Lune would stop, and think quickly about something else.

Clair-de-Lune admired her mother, the Perfect Dancer, deeply. But she feared that she would never be like her, for already she knew that there was something she wanted more than dancing. Clair-de-Lune would have given up anything—even dancing—to be able to speak.

Whereas, of course, for her mother, dancing was the most important thing of all.

How sad it was that one had to choose!

"This is your mother's anniversary, Clair-de-Lune," said her grandmother austerely. "So I want you to spend the rest of today thinking about how you might become more like her."

Clair-de-Lune nodded solemnly. But she blushed, although her grandmother did not notice.

"Now it is time for your errands," her grandmother concluded, handing her a list and a few coins.

Clair-de-Lune fetched her gray *pelisse* from the little trunk under her bed, collected her bonnet and the wicker shopping basket, kissed her grandmother, and set off.

Every afternoon, Clair-de-Lune went to the market in the street just outside, to buy what groceries her grandmother could afford. She also earned a little money by running errands for some of their neighbors. Sometimes, if she was lucky, this meant plums for tea, or an egg for breakfast. But usually only one or two people wanted something, and quite often nobody wanted anything at all. She would pause on each of the six floors on her way down the stairs and knock twice on each door.

"Nothing today, thank you, Clair-de-Lune," Miss Blossom, the singing teacher, would call in her plump, well-supported voice.

"Come back tomorrow," Mr. Kirk, the actor, would declaim with thrilling resonance.

"Oh . . . ," the flustered and elderly Mrs. Costello would say, scuttling to her door and opening it a crack, through which Minette would poke her inquisitive whiskered nose while her mistress fished in her purse for coins. "Would you get me a nice little bit of ladyfish? Only if it is fresh, mind! Thank you, my dear."

But from other doors, there would be no answer at all.

Clair-de-Lune had not been inside any other building since she was a baby, so she did not think her home peculiar. But any visitor seeing it for the first time would have been struck by its oddness. Each floor was different from every other. Some had unexpected landings or alcoves; some even had passages leading through to areas Clair-de-Lune had never visited, passages that would lead you briefly out into the open air and back inside again, for parts of the building had no roof! There were small, sudden stairways with doors at the top of them, and large, deep windows, some of them looking out on the street below or the theater opposite, others looking right into a wall of bricks. The fourth floor had a harpsichord on its landing that was never played. The second floor had an elaborate wicker chair.

Clair-de-Lune did not know it, but there was one floor in the building that she had never even seen, although she lived in the attic and had, she thought, to climb past every floor to reach it. But we shall hear more of that presently.

When Clair-de-Lune came out into the sunlight or the rain, the wind or the snow at last, it always seemed to her that she had stepped out of a prison. Sometimes she felt as if the building she lived in was simply everywhere—above her, below her, and anywhere she looked. Being out in the market on her own made her feel wild and free; she would skip from one stall to another, buying milk, bread, or fish from shop-keepers who were used to her silence, who understood her signs; then when the errands were done, she would walk a little way along the street, faster, faster, the groceries in her shopping basket banging against her legs as she looked hard around each corner, always hoping to see . . .

But no matter how far she walked—and she did not have time to walk far, for her grandmother would miss her—she never saw anything but buildings, one on top of the other, as far as the eye could see. Clair-de-Lune so longed to see some-thing beyond them that she always half expected that the landscape might change from day to day, and that on this day she might somehow catch a glimpse of a mountain, or the sea (which she knew was not far away), or a larger patch of sky that was not framed by the jagged edges of roofs. Sometimes she felt that she would burst if she did not see something that was free. But each day, when she reached the gateway of the church at the end of the street, she would pause, sigh, turn, then walk back slowly the way she had come. When she got to her doorway she would duck her head and go back inside. She would trudge up each of the twelve flights of stairs and pause on this floor or that to deliver her packages.

"Oh, thank you, my dear!" Mrs. Costello would say. "Minette will enjoy a nice morsel of fresh ladyfish for her tea. And I have a recipe for cream of ladyfish soup!"

Then Clair-de-Lune would make her way home to the attic, practice the piano, eat her supper, and go to bed.

On this particular afternoon, however, when Clair-de-Lune had finished her errands and was walking quickly along the street toward the church, absorbed in the events of that unusual day, she thought she heard a familiar giggle. It was not a suppressed giggle. It was one that wanted to be heard. She glanced immediately over to the opposite side of the street—and saw something that made her go hot and cold all over with shame.

Milly Twinkenham—the girl with the bright red hair and nut-brown eyes—and her friends Fenella Flynn and Prudence Eeling were walking along, arm in arm, directly opposite her, imitating her speed, manner, and gait.

Clair-de-Lune stopped walking immediately—her embarrassment and confusion froze her in her tracks. She looked at them for only a moment, only long enough to decide she must turn around and go home. But it was long enough to give Milly the opportunity to call out, "Yes? What? Is there something you want?"

And for Fenella and Prudence to laugh on cue.

Clair-de-Lune shook her head in panic and headed hurriedly back in the opposite direction. She could hear them, laughing still, behind her, and suspected there was something about her dress, or her bonnet, or her shopping basket that was drawing particular notice. She shrank into herself, trying her best to be less conspicuous, but thought that they must be able to see how strangely she was walking. It was because her legs were shaking so much.

When at last she ducked into her doorway, she leaned exhaustedly against the banister of the first flight of stairs, tears pricking at her eyes. She would never be able to take that little walk to the church again.

But then after a moment, quite suddenly, she remembered Bonaventure, and how he had promised to visit, and take her to the monastery.

And as she began the long climb up to the attic, something rose up in her that was so powerful it took her quite by surprise.

It wasn't shame or fear.

It was an utter determination not to give up.

For underneath it all, you see, Clair-de-Lune had a will of iron.

A Mouse Lullaby— and a Stone Door

That night, Clair-de-Lune dreamed a beautiful dream. She was standing on the ground floor of the building, and when she looked up she saw that the building was completely hollow—and that the uppermost ceiling was the night sky, full of stars!

The next morning, in the gray dawn, she was awoken by a tiny voice, singing.

> *Into the sailboat, my darling,*
> *And cuddle you up warm and deep*
> *And the Boat Mouse will take you a-sailing*
> *Across the Ocean of Sleep.*
> *Across the Ocean of Sleep, my dear!*
> *And the waves will rock you as I,*
> *Your mother-mouse, rock your cradle—*
> *Yet swift as the albatross fly.*

When you reach the Shore of Morning
I'll be waiting for you there
And the Island of Day
In the Ocean of Sleep
Will be fair as fair as fair!

Clair-de-Lune opened her eyes slowly. She could feel a tiny, damp, whiskery nose tickling her just below her ear. This sensation was at once strange and somehow familiar. *Whom do I know*, she thought sleepily, *with a nose like that?* Gently, she turned her head.

"Ah! Good morning, Mademoiselle Clair-de-Lune! I hope you do not object to being woken with a lullaby! It is not, I admit, entirely logical—to sing a lullaby just when I want to wake you up, I mean. But then, I wanted to wake you with especial solicitude, because I know that you are sad. Hardly the time for anything rousing. In fact, quite inappropriate, I would have thought. Now, before we set out—for I am offering my services to escort you to see my friend, Brother Inchmahome, if your leisure serves you now (and we must both be back in time for class!)—I must tell you something.

"When I crept in here not half a minute ago, my eye was caught immediately by a most beautiful sight—a silver bird with a glowing scarlet and gold heart roosting on your bedpost! I must say that I hoped to say hello to her and get a better look—but when, after scaling the difficult terrain of your bedclothes, I reached the summit of your bed (few people appreciate the athleticism of mice!), the bird woke and took fright and flew away, out the window.

"Was she yours? I hope she is not lost. But then, as you do not keep her in a cage (and very commendable, too—I do not hold with birds in cages), she must be used to coming and going. . . . Shall we go?"

Clair-de-Lune sat up carefully, so as not to disturb his position on the quilt. A bird? She did not understand, and could not ask him to explain. But even so, her heart had skipped a beat, as if he had just given her news of a long-lost friend.

Clair-de-Lune dressed quickly. She did not like to think of what her grandmother would say about this extraordinary expedition. But she had awoken with a new strength, a new clarity, a new certainty about what she had to do. No one she knew could help her. No one she knew even wanted to. But perhaps—by some miracle—someone she did not yet know could. . . .

The only thing she feared now was that her grandmother would awaken and stop her.

"Now follow me!" said the mouse when she was ready.

Across the attic floor they crept, past Clair-de-Lune's sleeping grandmother and out the door, onto the landing, Bonaventure swift and light, stopping and starting with dancer-mouse grace, Clair-de-Lune nervous and uncertain and stumbling, dancer though she was. Once outside the apartment, Clair-de-Lune closed the door so carefully that this stage of their departure seemed to take fully five minutes.

But her grandmother slept on.

So they began the long descent.

And here began, for Clair-de-Lune, a great and unexpected adventure.

Clair-de-Lune had been up and down these stairways many times, but she had never seen them so early in the morning. In the dim light of dawn, they looked different—so different that had she not been afraid of losing her guide (Bonaventure went very swiftly indeed, not attempting the stairs but sprinting, instead, athletically down the banisters), she would have paused to look more closely at what she thought she saw. For as she passed, she kept seeing things out of the corner of her eye that surely should not have been there at all.

Where there should have been a stair—a piece of damp rock?

Where there had always been an alcove—a cave, with moss?

At the end of a short passage, dimly—a waterfall?

Suddenly Clair-de-Lune had to stop, Bonaventure or no Bonaventure. She stood at the bottom of a staircase, steadied herself for a moment, then looked up.

Was it possible—could it be—

Was it dark gray cloudy dawn sky she saw above her, or just the distant ceiling?

"Mademoiselle!" Bonaventure was calling.

Clair-de-Lune looked down. In her confusion, she had lost track of how many stairways they had come down. Now she found herself on a floor she did not recognize. But how could that be? Had she not been to every floor in the building? Nevertheless, she knew she had never been here. For before her was a most beautiful stone door. It was very old, and exquisitely carved, and she knew she had never seen it in her life before.

Bonaventure beckoned to her. Then, all at once, he disappeared under the door, which ended some two inches above the floor. For a moment Clair-de-Lune thought that he expected her to do likewise. But then, slowly, the door swung open.

Clair-de-Lune Meets Brother Inchmahome

Clair-de-Lune fell back in astonishment.

Before her, running riotously up to the doorway, was a wild garden. Beyond that, a cliff edge. Beyond that, the sea! Above, the sky! And, a little to the right, the sheer gray face of a mountainside, into which there was carved—a monastery!

Clair-de-Lune shivered in the sudden fresh salt breeze.

"Come along, mademoiselle!" Bonaventure called shrilly, his tiny voice almost lost in the sounds of the sea below them and the garden—which was filled with birds—before them. "Follow me!"

Clair-de-Lune looked down at her feet. They stood on the worn boards of the passageway of this unfamiliar floor of the building. Directly in front of them, grass crept raggedly over the open doorway. She lifted her foot, placed it on the grass, and in three steps passed through the door. Immediately, she felt the gentle morning sun warm on her face. She was outside! Outside! But—

Her head was spinning. She shut her eyes. Then she looked behind her.

It seemed that she had just emerged from a cave. The damp gray rock around the entrance was jagged and mossy; the doorway, roughly oblong, was filled with a darkness so intense that she could see nothing beyond it. Indeed, the dark from which she seemed to have come was so black it almost frightened her.

Where was her home? Where was the building in which she had lived for most of her life? Could it be that it was somehow enclosed within a cave in a mountainside?

But where was she now? How could this sky, this sea, this garden, this mountain, this monastery hide themselves behind an old stone door?

But then, how could anything be really surprising in this strange world?

She turned again in wonder and followed Bonaventure's tiny form as he scurried through the grass, past wildflowers, past gnarled bushes and trees, past the cliffside and the blue, blue sea on her left, even more vast and free than she could have imagined, and with the hugeness of the sky above her wherever she looked.

Catching her breath with difficulty, she followed him up to the monastery door—carved, it seemed, into the mountainside—and waited, her heart thumping with astonishment, as he disappeared under it. Presently, the door opened, revealing an elderly monk with Bonaventure on his shoulder.

"You see," said Bonaventure to Clair-de-Lune, "I told you

the monastery was close by!" and, turning to the brother, "I have brought mademoiselle to see Brother Inchmahome. Please, where might he be found this morning?"

"He is in his study, Brother Mouse," said the old man, and he lowered the mouse gently to the floor, whereupon—before Clair-de-Lune even had time to curtsy politely to the monk— the mouse started confidently up the corridor, past a stone niche in which there stood the blue-robed statue of a lady, and past several deep windows cut into the rock, which looked out upon the sea.

But the old porter monk smiled at Clair-de-Lune's departing back, as if he knew her, or as if he had been expecting her for a long time.

At the end of the corridor there was an open door. Bonaventure hastened through it. Clair-de-Lune followed shyly and found herself in the doorway of a beautiful, book-lined stone room, with yet another open door leading out of it to a garden filled with flowers and herbs and ending in a sheer drop to the sea. In the center of the room, at a stone desk, there sat, very quietly, a man.

He was thin, this man, and fine-boned, with very dark, curly hair and perfectly gray eyes that half hid behind a small pair of spectacles. The crown of his head was shaved—for he was a monk—and he wore a monk's rough brown robe, tied at the waist with a rope, and brown sandals. His head was as beautifully shaped as a hen's egg: the line of his jaw was an artist's brushstroke, clean and fine, his chin was pointed—and dented in the middle—and he had an exceptionally high forehead

41

(as, indeed, does an egg), so his hair began to grow somewhat above the bump that was the top of his forehead, and a great distance above his eyes. His hair grew in two rounded peaks, which made his face, with its pointed chin, a heart. His skin, which was lightly tanned, had a gentle, warm flush, and—though he was clean-shaven—the stubble of his dark beard peppered the lower half of his face with an infinite number of tiny black dots. He had a long, intelligent-looking nose, a generous mouth, and large white teeth. His face was pleasant, beautiful, and mild. But it was perhaps his expression that was most striking; that and his eyes. There was something about the grayness of them—neither blue-gray nor green-gray, but the gray of water flowing over stone—something about the clearness of them, something about the way they half hid, shyly, behind his spectacles. As for his expression . . .

He was deeply engaged, at this moment, in the contemplation of a large, smooth, oval pebble that sat on the desk before him. He had a big ledger open beside it, and the page under his thin hand was already half filled with tiny, scribbly, spidery handwriting; but now he had stopped writing, and sat gazing at the stone with an immensely calm, happy expression on his face. It was as if he thought he was looking at the most beautiful thing in the world.

This was Brother Inchmahome, whose eyes always seemed to be looking at the most beautiful thing in the world.

Apart from the books, the room was very bare, but the gray stone of its walls and floor and furniture was so beautiful, the garden beyond it so exquisite, and Brother Inchmahome so calm and happy that Clair-de-Lune thought it was the loveli-est place she had ever seen.

Meanwhile, Bonaventure had climbed up Brother Inchmahome's arm and was nuzzling him, in his whiskery way, below the ear. Brother Inchmahome did not move. With his eyes on the pebble, he said, in a mild, kind, humorous voice:

"Good morning, Bonaventure."

"Brother Inchmahome," said the mouse, "I have brought someone to meet you. She is a wonderful dancer—she dances as well as a mouse!—and yet she is sad. What a terrible mys-tery, don't you agree? And yet I know you—who are interested in everyone and everything, and are incomparably wise—can solve it!"

Brother Inchmahome laughed.

"Ah, Bonaventure," he said, "you flatter me, Brother Mouse!" And he stroked the mouse's head gently with his index finger. Then, leaving his contemplation of the pebble with a little sigh of regret, he turned alertly to Clair-de-Lune. "Well, mademoiselle, after such an introduction you are bound to be disappointed. . . ." Then, all at once, he began to look at Clair-de-Lune in something of the manner that he had been looking at the pebble. "Is it true that you are sad? Ah, but I can see that it is! Might I ask why?"

Clair-de-Lune looked back at Brother Inchmahome in won-der. She had never before been looked at through eyes like his. Everyone else she knew looked at her as if they already knew what they were going to find—her grandmother, Monsieur Dupoint, the other students, even dear Bonaventure, who had been so friendly and funny and kind. But Brother Inchmahome looked at her as if he had just discovered an entirely new country, whose mountains and rivers, plants and animals, weather and dangers were as yet uncharted. He seemed profoundly interested in what he was about to discover, no matter what it turned out to be. And it seemed to Clair-de-Lune—who, it must be remembered, had just discovered a mountain, a sea, and a sky all inside the building—that this was the most extraordinary thing she had seen all morning.

Faced with such interest, she scarcely knew what to do. But before she had time to feel awkward, Brother Inchmahome spoke again.

"Ah!" he said softly. "You are sad because you cannot speak!"

Clair-de-Lune's eyes widened with astonishment.

Bonaventure was jumping around the desk and squeaking. He was so excited that his mousy accent became almost too pronounced for Clair-de-Lune to be able to make out the words.

"Ah, what a fool of a mouse I am!" he squeaked. "Why did I not think of that? Mademoiselle cannot speak! Indeed, what a terrible infirmity! Even dancing, to be sure, could not make up for that. Or not quite, anyway. You see how wise he is?" he added proudly to Clair-de-Lune, calming down slightly.

"Oh, that is not wisdom!" said Brother Inchmahome. "That is listening. And you, my dear Bonaventure," he added sternly, "are no fool at all, as I hope you know." For a moment, he turned to the mouse with such intense interest that Clair-de-Lune felt sad, fearing that she had been abandoned already.

But almost immediately he turned back to her. "Mademoiselle, I must tell you something. Do you know that the brothers here are silent as much as possible, and that during the night—from the end of the last prayer in the evening till the beginning of the first prayer the next morning—the silence may be broken only in cases of dire necessity? We call that the Great Silence. Silence can be a good thing, you know, partly because it helps one to listen. Silence can say more than a thousand words. And words—alas!" He gestured toward the ledger, its open page half filled with his tiny, spidery handwriting, in which he had been trying to describe the pebble. "Words cannot say everything. Sometimes, indeed, I think they can say nothing of real worth. Mademoiselle, speaking is not necessary."

Clair-de-Lune was so disappointed that she smiled in order to hide her feelings. She felt that to show them to such a kindly man would have been the height of rudeness.

"Ah," said Brother Inchmahome gently, "but it is necessary to you!"

Again Clair-de-Lune was astonished. She stared at him, her mouth slightly open.

"You want to speak," he murmured happily, half to himself. "And I long to listen!"

Her mouth still open, Clair-de-Lune blinked.

"Well, then," he went on a little more briskly. "Would you like me to help you—to speak?"

Clair-de-Lune went pale with delight.

Brother Inchmahome smiled broadly.

Clair-de-Lune gave one nod, but the nod was so deep it seemed for a moment that she might overbalance.

Brother Inchmahome laughed.

"Now," he said when she had recovered a little, "I will share with you a secret. I think you can speak already. Ah, mademoiselle, hear me out!" Clair-de-Lune had begun earnestly to shake her head in protest. "You see, I think that all you need is for someone to listen to you. And I would be more than happy to be that someone. After all, what is the point of speaking if nobody is listening?

"Mademoiselle—er, pardon me, what is your name?"

"Clair-de-Lune!" cried Bonaventure promptly.

"Moonlight!" said Brother Inchmahome. He paused for a moment, his gray eyes dreamy, as if he was thinking of some happy—or perhaps sad—memory. Then he sighed and resumed gently, "Your mother must be a poetic person, to name you so—ah, but she is in heaven, is she not?" Again he had guessed! "I am sorry. Perhaps one day soon, you will tell me about her.

"Mademoiselle Clair-de-Lune, I have made it my life's work to listen to and observe as many things as possible in as minute and truthful detail as possible, for it seems to me that to do this is to love them and to love their Creator. Once, long ago, I felt all alone in the world. But then I understood that to listen is to know that we are not alone. I have listened to many silent things, and many silent things, in their kindness, have spoken to me. If you want to speak, here I will be, listening. But even if you are silent, I will hear.

"Now, I propose that you visit the monastery every morning at this hour. A short lesson every day is all that is needed. But now I must ask—does anyone know that you are here?"

Clair-de-Lune shook her head. Ordinarily, this state of affairs would have worried her considerably. But she was so happy she could not bring herself to worry.

"Well, then—whom might you ask for permission to visit the monastery?"

"Her grandmama," said Bonaventure. "Or perhaps her teacher, Monsieur Dupoint."

"Then before you come back tomorrow, you must ask permission of either of those good people. But before you go, here is a question. I am sending you away, mademoiselle, to meditate upon it!

"Why is it, do you think, that you cannot speak?"

Bonaventure had departed for the morning and was already halfway down the hall. "Till tomorrow, Brother!" Clair-de-Lune heard him squeak. All his appearances and departures, it seemed, were abrupt like this. But Clair-de-Lune stood for a moment, not wanting to leave. Suddenly life on the other side of the stone door seemed unbearably sad. *And what,* she thought, panicking suddenly, *if this is a dream?*

"This is no dream," said Brother Inchmahome in a voice that mocked her gently for worrying. "I will be here tomorrow. You are a pessimist, I see, mademoiselle! Ah, but I am an optimist, and so I say, do not fear! The world is not nearly so treacherous as you suspect—and a great deal more wonderful!" His clear gray eyes, gray as pebbles, clear as water, smiled at her.

Clair-de-Lune looked once more about the stone room and at the garden beyond it, and sighed. Then, looking first for a moment into the monk's eyes to impress upon him the meaning of her action, she performed a most beautiful *révérence*—a dancer's curtsy—bowing her head. This was to say, with all her heart, *Thank you*. Then she ran after Bonaventure.

Back they went, the mouse and the child, past the statue of the lady, past the porter monk, and out the door, over the grass, through the sunshine, past the sea and the flowers and herbs, under the vast sky toward the door of black darkness, the cave, that led back into the strange building, stranger than anyone could have imagined, that was Clair-de-Lune's home. Clair-de-Lune had been afraid to come out here. Now she was afraid to go back. But Bonaventure was a mouse. He was used to danger. She took a deep breath and followed him blindly into the dark.

On the other side, the stone door closed itself gently behind them, as if blown by a secret breeze. Clair-de-Lune peered into the gloom about her.

"Do not worry," said Bonaventure. "I have been back many times. It is always here. Now you must go home, and so must I, and we must both prepare for class. I will come and fetch you tomorrow! *Adieu!*" and he was gone, haring off down the banister.

Clair-de-Lune began slowly to climb the stairs. *What will Grandmama say?* she thought with some trepidation, for surely the old lady would be awake by now. She was so preoccupied with this that she lost track of how many flights she had come up before realizing that again she was on the attic floor. Clair-de-Lune stopped. *How could that be?* she thought, looking back down the way she had come and seeing nothing unfamiliar. Then she noticed the light, for she was standing next to a window, through which she could see red-tiled roofs and chimneys as far as the eye could see—and a jagged square of the gray dawn sky. No time seemed to have passed at all.

Silently, Clair-de-Lune crept back into the attic, past her sleeping grandmother, and, undressing quickly, got back into bed. Surely it *had* been a dream.

Clair-de-Lune Does Not Ask

Nevertheless, all through her class with Monsieur Dupoint that morning, she thought about Brother Inchmahome's question.

Why was it that she could not speak?

And when she was not thinking of that, she was thinking with joy and delight and wonder of Brother Inchmahome and the monastery and the cliff and the sea and the sky that were hidden upstairs—or was it downstairs?—in the very building where she had felt so confined.

And when she was not thinking of that, she was worrying about asking permission.

Happiness had stopped her worrying at first. Now worry was creeping back in, like a cold little hand.

"Pay attention, Clair-de-Lune!" remonstrated Monsieur Dupoint as Clair-de-Lune pointed the wrong foot. He spoke in the slightly shocked tone of one who had expected better. Two or three of the girls in the class tittered, pleased that the pet was temporarily out of favor.

Startled, Clair-de-Lune blushed and corrected herself.

How surprised Monsieur Dupoint would have been if he could have witnessed the scene taking place within Bonaventure's mouse hole. For, of course, every morning, like Clair-de-Lune, Bonaventure did Monsieur Dupoint's class. But—much as he respected Monsieur Dupoint as a teacher and former *danseur* of renown—he was most upset when he heard that gentleman reproving his friend. Immediately, he abandoned his *grands battements* and scurried to the door of his mouse hole to see what was going on. And—although of course quite invisibly to the parties concerned—he shook his tiny mouse fist toward the unfortunate ballet master and threatened dire consequences should these unfair remonstrations continue. "The child is learning to speak!" he squeaked indignantly. "What does it matter what foot she was pointing? Whatever foot she chooses to point, she points divinely!" Afterward, however, he calmed down and forgave Monsieur Dupoint for what was, after all, quite reasonable behavior from a strict ballet master.

Now, when Clair-de-Lune really needed to say something, she was of course able to write a note. Had her grandmother been more encouraging of conversation, Clair-de-Lune might have spent a lot of time writing letters. But of course she was not, for letters, Clair-de-Lune's grandmother believed, created friends—not to mention lovers—almost more effectively than speech. (Indeed, there had been many desperate letters between La Lune and the disreputable young man.) So Clair-de-Lune used this method only in cases of dire necessity.

As luck would have it, at the end of the class, when he had

dismissed them all, Monsieur Dupoint said, "Excuse me, Mr. Sparrow—I must discuss with you the tempo of that excerpt from *Giselle* which we use for the little *enchaînement* we are working on," and in consultation with Mr. Sparrow at the piano he scribbled some notes on the music. Clair-de-Lune knew that she could borrow pencil and paper and write him a short note, asking permission to visit the monastery.

She hesitated.

"Clair-de-Lune!" said Monsieur Dupoint, looking up. "Still here? Do not lose heart, my child—we dancers all have our off days. Eat a hearty luncheon—you seem thin to me—and go early to bed. I look forward to seeing my old Clair-de-Lune again tomorrow!"

Clair-de-Lune curtsied and made her escape. Well, she could ask her grandmother instead. But she knew that Monsieur Dupoint would have been easier.

At lunch (alas, only bread and weak black tea and a sliver of sausage), Clair-de-Lune tried to ask her grandmother for permission to visit the monastery. She tried also at the beginning of lessons, at the end of lessons, and when she came back from running her errands. But each time her courage failed her.

"Good night, child," said her grandmother finally, after a supper of bread and milk and a morsel of ladyfish (smaller than Minette's) poached in their fish kettle.

As for the answer to Brother Inchmahome's question . . .

Why was it that she could not speak?

Clair-de-Lune could find no answer.

She was not happy anymore. Now she was sad, for it

seemed to her that even though Brother Inchmahome was the most remarkable person she had ever met, even though there was a cliff and a sea and a sky—and a monastery!—all hidden, secret, within the building, she was going to fail. She could not learn to speak, and that was that.

Beginners, Please!

But not everyone was discouraged that night. For meanwhile, in the mouse hole three floors below, by the light of a tiny stump of discarded birthday candle, Bonaventure was working.

In the short time since he had adopted Clair-de-Lune as a friend, he had regarded the task of escorting her to Brother Inchmahome as a Sacred Duty.

But he had not allowed it to put him behind with his schedule. For his dream—that of a ballet exclusively for mice—was a Sacred Duty also.

At that moment, he was preparing his first class.

It was hard work, and required a good deal of imagination.

First he would pretend to be himself, as teacher, standing out in front, explaining and demonstrating an exercise for his imaginary class. He was careful to speak audibly and to maintain imaginary eye contact.

Then he would scuttle back to a position toward the middle of the room, turn to face the opposite direction, and pretend to be a pupil trying to do what he had just said. He tried to imagine the kinds of difficulties this imaginary pupil might encounter, and to remember what he himself had found most challenging when first observing Monsieur Dupoint's classes.

Then he would return to the front of the room, turn around again, demonstrate more clearly, and explain more fully. He was careful to add encouragement and not to become impatient with himself.

Then he would rush to the tiny notebook he kept open on the floor and, lying on his stomach, scribble some tiny notes.

He felt much indebted to Monsieur Dupoint, who had, unwittingly, taught him how to teach. The ballet master could not have done it better if he had known the mouse was there. But Bonaventure was also aware that certain adaptations would be needed, in order that Monsieur Dupoint's style of teaching be truly beneficial to a class of mice.

Still, creativity was Bonaventure's strong point.

There was also the fact that his students—not to mention he as their teacher—would be absolute beginners, without even the vaguest precedent to guide them. For no one, to Bonaventure's knowledge, had ever before, in the history of the art, taught classical ballet to mice.

And yet, Bonaventure felt equal to it—along with a suitable degree of humility. Confidence—tempered with respect— was also a strong point of his.

The mouse hole was looking less and less like the home of a mouse who happened to be a *balletomane,* and more and more like a dancing school for mice. Bonaventure had been collecting discarded theatrical handbills for some time. (This was easy for a mouse who lived in a building opposite a theater.) Over the last few days he had been painstakingly cutting out from them beautiful pictures of famous dancers and tacking them up above the mirrors around the mouse hole. He had also put up two pocket handkerchiefs (lost, mind you, and unclaimed—Bonaventure's mother had always impressed upon him the difference between a mouse and a thief) to divide the two back corners into dressing rooms, one for males and one for females. The handkerchiefs were both white, and somewhat ink-stained, and embroidered with the monogram CD. Bonaventure rather wished the initials were the other way round. Then he could have imagined they stood for "dancing class" rather than being, as they were, merely the initials of a certain Charles Dickens.

The previous week, Bonaventure had designed a beautiful poster announcing the establishment of his school, and the date and time of the commencement of classes. This he had taken to a mouse friend of his by the name of Leonard, who lived with his wife and daughter in a print shop and who had become expert in the illicit use of the printing press for mouse purposes. (Leonard was in fact engaged in the production of the first *Collected Works of Shakespeare* to be printed especially for mice.) The next morning, Bonaventure had a hundred posters, and he had spent a day or two putting these up at mouse-eye level all over the building and around the nearby streets. They were, of course, too small for any humans to see—unless they were looking very hard. But mice saw them, and told their friends. Before long every mouse in the building knew that Bonaventure was starting a dancing school especially for mice—and the news was spreading further, for the mouse grapevine is vast and efficient.

Bonaventure would have been most gratified had he witnessed a scene that had taken place only that morning in front of a poster he had put up, daringly, near the entrance to the theater.

"Oh, Rudolph, look!" a young female mouse had exclaimed upon catching sight of the poster. She was white as snow, wore a pink ribbon tied at a fetching angle around her neck, and had exceptionally expressive whiskers, which were twitching with excitement. "A ballet school especially for mice! It's what we've been waiting for!"

"Is it?" said her fiancé, Rudolph, to whose arm she clung prettily. "Well, you would know, my dear."

"How I have always longed to perform—in a suitably lady-like manner, of course. But there are so few opportunities for mice! And then there is you, my love, and your jumps, which are quite wasted from an artistic point of view, even if they have got you out of a few tight spots. We must enroll together, Rudolph!"

"Must we, Margot?" Rudolph inquired, pushing his spectacles, which were always slipping, back toward his eyes, and peering doubtfully at the poster.

"Of course we must, my dear. I am thinking of your talents even more than mine. Ballet is all about jumps, for males. Just wait till they see you!"

"Just wait until they see *you*," returned Rudolph gallantly, and they continued on their way in a somewhat canoodling fashion. They were engaged, after all.

They were Bonaventure's first two pupils, and they enrolled that very afternoon.

The First Answer

When Clair-de-Lune felt Bonaventure's whiskery nose beneath her ear the next morning, she was already half awake, having slept badly. She scarcely knew if she should follow Bonaventure at all—could she go back when she had not done what Brother Inchmahome had asked? But the idea of not visiting him—of perhaps never seeing him again, of him wondering what had become of her—gave her such pain that she knew she had to go, if only to explain. She dressed quickly and offered Bonaventure her hand—for now that she knew the way, it seemed harsh that he should walk when he could ride. She cradled him next to her chest, and felt his furry warmth and his tiny heartbeat and his whiskery nose peeking out over her fingers.

"Much obliged, I'm sure!" he said.

Then she crept past her sleeping grandmother, out onto the landing, and down the stairs.

She was taking the stairs so carefully—for when you are carrying someone you have to be careful—that again she lost track of how many flights she had gone down before she reached the floor with the stone door. But as soon as she placed her foot on the landing, it opened—as if just for her!—and all at once, before she could see anything beyond the brightness of the morning light, she could hear the lovely murmur of the sea.

Because she was sad, because she feared she might never see them again, the wild garden, the mountain, and the sky seemed even more beautiful than they had yesterday.

"He is in the sea garden," said the porter when Bonaventure asked, and so they walked down the hall (passing two young monks—novices—who smiled at them kindly), through the study, and out into the sea garden, with its herbs and flowers and its sheer drop to the wide, blue sea.

"There he is!" said Bonaventure happily.

But when Clair-de-Lune saw the monk, she stopped in wonder.

Brother Inchmahome was sitting in the sunlight on a stone bench facing the sea, his figure illuminated in the early morning light like the chapter heading of an ancient manuscript. He was scribbling, in his funny, spidery handwriting, into his ledger, which sat on his knees. His brown robes, his dark curly hair, and the pages of his ledger stirred faintly in the breeze, but apart from his writing Brother Inchmahome was very still. Every so often, in a slight, graceful movement, he would look up and sit quietly for a moment, calm and yet alert, his head inclined as if listening. Then, his face intent, he would scribble some more. Was it the sea he was listening to? Or was he listening to everything?

Brother Inchmahome's calmness and peace, his listening, was so powerful that it seemed to Clair-de-Lune that she could see it filling the air about him, as would warmth or light. When she had come out into the garden she had been sad and anxious; now, just looking at him, she felt calm and forgiven. And yet she hesitated, not wishing to disturb him. For after all, it was *his* warmth, *his* light, and she did not know if she belonged there.

But Bonaventure had no such hesitance. As soon as he saw the monk, he sprang gaily out of her hands, across the grass, and up onto the stone seat, where he nibbled mousily at Brother Inchmahome's fingers in greeting, then ran up his arm and settled himself on his shoulder. Brother Inchmahome smiled as he wrote, and reached up a finger to stroke the little mouse.

"Ah, Bonaventure!" he said. "And Clair-de-Lune . . ." He wrote a few more words, shut the ledger, placed it on the bench beside him, and turned his kind, heart-shaped face toward her. "May I call you Clair-de-Lune? Have you asked your grandmother? And have you an answer to my question?"

Clair-de-Lune hung her head. But just as, sadly, she was about to raise her head and shake it . . .

She knew the answer.

Clair-de-Lune's face lit up. Brother Inchmahome smiled back at her. "What?" he said.

But then Clair-de-Lune remembered that she could not speak. And what was the use of her knowing the answer if she could not tell him?

She looked at him hopelessly.

"Ah," said Brother Inchmahome, looking at her mildly and cheerfully from behind his spectacles, "but you forget. I think you can speak already—or will be able to if I listen."

Then, completely calm and yet brightly alert, he simply sat there listening.

How Clair-de-Lune wanted to speak!

She opened her mouth. She licked her lips. She took a breath. She took another. But no matter how she tried, it seemed to her that she just could not. She didn't know how.

Tears filled her eyes and, softly, overflowed.

But Brother Inchmahome did not look sad. He just looked interested.

"Make any noise," he suggested. "Any noise at all."

Clair-de-Lune swallowed, looked away, looked back at him, closed her eyes. She tried to make a noise. She tried to make another. She began to shake her head—

Then she heard it, or felt it, or sensed it, not only around Brother Inchmahome, but around her, Clair-de-Lune: the warm silence, full of light, that was Brother Inchmahome's listening.

It was holding her to stop her falling.

She opened her mouth . . . and a tiny sound—a noise, barely audible—arose from somewhere inside her.

Her eyes flew open, wide with surprise and alarm.

But Brother Inchmahome only smiled cheerfully at her. It struck her suddenly that he was enjoying himself.

"Now!" he said. "Just think what you want to say to me, and make a sound at the same time."

Clair-de-Lune looked at him apprehensively. She could

hardly believe what was happening. She was half elated and half afraid.

She took a deep breath and again closed her eyes.

I did not ask my grandmama, she thought, *because I was afraid she would say no. You see, she would not wish me to come here, because she wants me to stay mute. And that, Brother Inchmahome, is why I cannot speak. I do not have my grandmama's permission.*

As she thought this, she made noises as soft as a baby bird's. They sounded like a baby talking, before a baby can talk. They sounded like this:

"Ah . . . ah ah ah . . . ah! Ah-ah, ah, ah, ah . . . ah!"

Clair-de-Lune fell silent, then sighed deeply. Suddenly she felt exhausted and sad, for she knew that *that* was not speaking. How could it be speaking if no one could understand it?

She looked apologetically at Brother Inchmahome.

But she found she did not understand the expression on his face. Strangely, he appeared to be considering what he had just heard, almost as if he had understood it.

"How very singular!" he observed, looking at her with profound interest.

But . . . ! thought Clair-de-Lune.

"Could it be," wondered Brother Inchmahome, "that your grandmother does not think speaking a good thing?"

But . . . ! thought Clair-de-Lune.

"And yet," mused Brother Inchmahome, "she speaks herself, does she not?"

But . . . ! thought Clair-de-Lune.

"In any case, Clair-de-Lune," said Brother Inchmahome

seriously, "she must not stop you, even if she is your grandmother. You have a right to speak, you know . . . given to you by God himself! No one, not even your good grandmother—for I'm sure she is a good person underneath—" he muttered to himself, "has any right to take what God has given."

Clair-de-Lune stared at him in astonishment. He had understood! But how was this possible? It was not possible! It was—

"You are surprised that I understand you?" said Brother Inchmahome gently.

Clair-de-Lune was trembling. She nodded passionately.

"Ah, but Clair-de-Lune—you make perfect sense! When will you believe me, my dear? It is only a matter of listening."

All this time, Bonaventure had been sitting reverently in the grass at Brother Inchmahome's feet. Now he jumped up and clasped his little paws ardently on his breast. "Listening?" he exclaimed. "But surely, Brother Inchmahome, this listening you speak of is a miraculous thing!"

Then Brother Inchmahome grew dreamy, and though his eyes looked kindly down at the little mouse, it was as if he were seeing something much farther away.

"A miraculous thing?" he said. "Perhaps it is. And yet, it is only listening, and surely everyone should be able to do that. We all have ears. I have thought a great deal about this, for I have spent years trying to learn how to do it. It is difficult—or was for me. You have to let what you are listening to be whatever it wants to be . . . and the funny thing is, you see, that at first this is frightening. Perhaps that is because—" Then he stopped, looking suddenly shy. "But you don't want to hear about this . . . do you?"

If Clair-de-Lune had been more used to making herself heard, she might have said immediately, *Yes, of course, please tell us about listening,* but Brother Inchmahome hurried on, "And Clair-de-Lune is tired, I can see. That is enough for one day. Except—I want to give you another task.

"Clair-de-Lune, that is not the only reason you cannot speak. Think of another . . . and tell me tomorrow.

"And now," he added, pulling on the brown cloak that lay on the seat beside him, "I am coming home with you to ask your grandmama. You see, I am not afraid!"

He reached down and offered his hand to Bonaventure, who immediately climbed onto it. Then he held out his other hand to Clair-de-Lune. She took it, smiling shyly, and the three companions set out, leaving the garden, passing through the study and back through the hall, past the porter, to whom Brother Inchmahome nodded and smiled, out through the door, and through the wild garden toward the cave that was the doorway back into the building.

Clair-de-Lune had to trot to keep up, for Brother Inchmahome walked purposefully, and with big strides. But she felt proud, and honored, to be walking beside him, and suddenly it was not sad or frightening to have to go back through the black doorway—indeed, it was thrilling to do so with a friend. When they passed through it, she almost laughed—but not quite, for Clair-de-Lune could not laugh out loud any more than she could cry.

But Bonaventure heard her.

"Pray, what amuses you, mademoiselle?" he asked from Brother Inchmahome's shoulder, his whiskers twitching inquisitively.

"Ah," said Brother Inchmahome. "That, if I'm not mistaken, was a very quiet—indeed, silent!—little laugh of joy, my dear Bonaventure. And now, Brother Mouse, as it seems that our paths lead in opposite directions, it is time for us to say good morning!"

"Good morning indeed!" agreed Bonaventure, who was already halfway down the stairs. "Until tomorrow, Brother, mademoiselle!"

And there they stood, Clair-de-Lune and Brother Inchmahome, on the dark landing with the stone door closing behind them. But the dark was lit up by Brother Inchmahome's presence.

"Which way?" he said, and so Clair-de-Lune led him up the stairs to the attic—and this time she was far too distracted by having Brother Inchmahome with her to notice how many flights she had climbed. But when she reached the landing outside the attic and saw the window, she remembered for the first time that of course, as yesterday, no time had passed—and thus her grandmother would still be asleep. Outside the window it was barely dawn. How could he ask her now? She turned to look questioningly at him and saw that his face had grown dreamy again.

"How easy it is to forget," he said faintly, "about the world out here. . . ."

Then he saw that she was worried about her grandmother.

"She has not yet arisen?" he said absently. "No, of course . . . Never mind—I will wait here until she is ready to see me."

He paused, looking about him.

"Now my listening will be tested," he murmured after a moment. "Yes! It is hard to listen to everything, and to let everything, even painful things, be whatever they want to be. . . . You go back to bed, Clair-de-Lune," he added kindly. "You have worked hard this morning, and need your rest!"

Clair-de-Lune hesitated. Should she really allow him to wait here for an hour or more? But already, she knew, he was listening to something, something he could hear but she could not. She sighed. He had forgotten her already. She opened the door to the attic—and then closed it again quietly. She leaned over and pulled gently on his sleeve to attract his attention. She looked seriously into his eyes for a moment, then performed a *révérence* that was even more beautiful than yesterday's (for a dancer's curtsy can be very elaborate). *Thank you, Brother Inchmahome.*

He smiled gravely and bowed his head in return. "You're very welcome, Clair-de-Lune."

Then, bursting with happiness, she disappeared into the attic.

Clair-de-Lune would never have believed that she could sleep in such circumstances. But she was so tired, and she felt so safe knowing that Brother Inchmahome was waiting outside the door—and, somehow, so certain that he belonged there—that soon, in the chill gray dawn, she fell into a deep, happy sleep.

Brother Inchmahome Is Still There

By the time Clair-de-Lune woke up, she had forgotten all about the events of the early morning.

"Wake up, child! Hurry and dress yourself! We have both overslept, and you must not be late. A dancer is never late."

Ordinarily, Clair-de-Lune would have been miserable at such an awakening. But this morning she was so happy that she jumped out of bed, got dressed, and ate as quickly as possible, with giggles bubbling up inside her that almost—but never quite—burst out into sound. It was somehow funny to have overslept. It was somehow funny that her grandmother was so deeply displeased by it.

"Straighten your back, child—where are your feet? And—good heavens, girl, what are you thinking of?—*cease that smirking immediately!* What has got into you this morning? Dancers *do not* smirk!"

And of course that was even funnier. A smirking ballerina! But Clair-de-Lune cast her eyes down gravely.

"Now be off with you. You should be just in time."

Clair-de-Lune fell out the door, and there, on the window seat, still waiting, with an immensely calm and happy expression on his face, was Brother Inchmahome.

All at once Clair-de-Lune remembered.

And all at once her heart was pierced with a happiness that was almost pain.

She wanted to say something to him, but she did not know what it was. So she thought simply, *You're still here!* and made a noise like a purr in her throat.

"Of course I am," he said. Then he nodded goodbye to her, got up, brushed down his habit with the air of one who had just finished a long and complicated journey, drew himself up, and knocked on the attic door.

"Who is it?" came Clair-de-Lune's grandmother's stern, surprised voice.

And Clair-de-Lune fled down the stairs.

Clair-de-Lune never did find out what Brother Inchmahome said to her grandmother. All she knew was that at noon, when she arrived home for lunch (after a morning of worry and wonder and yet another remonstration from Monsieur Dupoint—not to mention more imperceptible fist-shaking from Bonaventure), her grandmother was in an extremely absent and disconcerted mood. What's more, when Clair-de-Lune was halfway through her first slice of bread, she announced, rather as if she expected Clair-de-Lune not to like it:

"A Brother Inchmahome was here from the monastery. He has offered to give you instruction in the Expression of the Soul, a discipline that he says is vital for artists. I have agreed—on the condition that these lessons do not interfere with your normal studies—as it seems to me that visiting the monastery would be a Steadying Influence. You will go every morning at six o'clock, when the good brother has a short space of leisure. In payment you will run errands for the brothers."

Thus it was that Clair-de-Lune gained her grandmother's permission to learn to speak, although she was never entirely sure that her grandmother grasped exactly what Brother Inchmahome meant by the Expression of the Soul.

But there was something else Clair-de-Lune didn't know. Her grandmother had been familiar for many years with a story that there was a monastery in the building. But she had always believed it to be a legend.

That morning's lesson had not been easy for Clair-de-Lune. First there were her absentminded mistakes and Monsieur Dupoint's irritation and the feeling that the rest of the class was quite happy for her to be in trouble.

Then, when it was over, there was Milly Twinkenham.

Clair-de-Lune was so preoccupied with this and that—and no wonder!—that she did not notice the gaggle of girls at the back of the classroom until she was almost upon them. They were crowding around something: what?

Could it be . . . ?

Clair-de-Lune stopped still in fright, for they were very near Bonaventure's mouse hole.

But they were not looking downward. They were looking

at something on the wall. They would be silent for a moment as Milly leaned toward it; then suddenly, as she stood back, they would burst out into giggles.

Clair-de-Lune felt uneasy, but she knew now that Bonaventure was not in danger, and she did not want to be noticed if she could help it. Before she managed to pass through the door, however, Milly saw her.

"Oh, Clair-de-Lune," she called, her voice trembling. She was shaking with giggles and holding something—was it a pencil?—in her hand. Suddenly her companions were silent, watching. "Come over here."

She seemed almost friendly. Clair-de-Lune hesitated, took a few steps toward her, then stopped, standing uncertainly before them.

Something about her must have set them off. Suddenly, looking at her, they all began to laugh.

They laughed and laughed as, confused, her face flaming, Clair-de-Lune stood irresolute, facing them. If only she could speak! If only she could say something—ask them what was funny, explain to them that she was not silent by choice!

But she could not, and so, trying desperately to act as if she had not been humiliated, as if they had not laughed at her, trying as hard as she could to move calmly and with dignity, she crept away.

"*Mesdemoiselles!*" said Monsieur Dupoint sharply from the piano. "What do you think my classroom is—a common *café*? I will not have silly girls giggling in that empty-headed manner while I am attempting to discuss music with Mr. Sparrow.

You are dancers—*artistes*! You should be meditating reverently on the class you have just done! Out! Out at once!" And he clapped his hands as if scaring off cats.

That evening, in the twilight, as her grandmother dozed uneasily over a stern little book, Clair-de-Lune leaned out the attic window, gazed at the lights of the city below, and thought again about Brother Inchmahome's question.

She also thought about the answer she had given and, as she thought, felt that she understood it more clearly. It was not just that her grandmother thought it better that she did not speak. It was not even that her grandmother did not want her to speak. It was that her grandmother had so little interest in speaking—gave it so little weight in comparison to the things she felt Really Mattered—that Clair-de-Lune had always found it difficult to believe that she had a right even to wish to do such a frivolous thing, no matter how necessary it seemed to her.

The truth was that until she had met Brother Inchmahome, she had known no one who thought it important that she learn to speak.

Then a strange thought occurred to her.

What about her mother? Would she have wanted her to learn to speak?

Clair-de-Lune went suddenly still with the intensity of the thought.

Immediately, pictures came into her head of the beautiful La Lune in her swan costume, her large, dark eyes gazing out rapturously at the portrait painter. She tried to picture that lady living with her grandmother and Clair-de-Lune herself in the attic, and being familiar with the fact of Clair-de-Lune's muteness—but somehow, it was impossible to fit her in. For that La Lune lived in the scrapbook on top of the cupboard.

But then a more shadowy picture came into her head, of La Lune in an ordinary day dress, talking, laughing, darning her *pointe* shoes.

And then suddenly Clair-de-Lune was afraid, for it seemed to her that she could hear that strange voice again, muffled by many layers of—she did not know what—trying more insistently than ever before to talk to her, to tell her something horrible, something she did not want to hear, and she was flooded with such a confusion of feelings that she had to stop thinking about it, for fear—for fear—

For fear of—she did not know what.

Clair-de-Lune calmed herself.

It took longer than usual.

One day, perhaps, she thought at last, *I will try to tell Brother Inchmahome about this. Perhaps he will tell me how I might send it away. But for now I must answer his question.*

Why is it that I cannot speak?

Clair-de-Lune settled herself anew and began to think carefully about what it felt like whenever she tried to speak. She thought about the time—only two days ago, although it felt much longer—when she had tried to speak to Mr. Sparrow, and what she had felt like before she had begun making her baby-bird noises to Brother Inchmahome.

She knew words: she could read and write. She understood what other people said to her. She could form sentences to say in her head. But every time she tried to say them out loud, something stopped her: a thing that felt like a hand in her throat, a hand made of iron. At the same time—just at the point where it felt as if a word might be about to escape—she felt afraid, too afraid to allow the word to be said.

Why am I afraid? she asked herself.

And the answer came immediately into her head.

Caverns, Dark Valleys, and Sea Bottoms

Clair-de-Lune took a deep breath. Then she said to Brother Inchmahome in the baby-bird voice that only he could understand:

I'm afraid of what I might say.

The monk, the mouse, and the young girl were sitting in the sunlight in the wild garden, the garden in front of the monastery. There had been no need to ask the porter where Brother Inchmahome was this morning. They had almost fallen over him as they came through the door. He had been lying full length on his stomach, listening to a blade of grass. Now, as he sat with them on his voluminous brown cloak, which he had spread out for them like a picnic blanket, the front of his habit was beaded with dew. All around them on the damp grass were small white flowers like stars. Above them, tiny swallows dipped and swooped against the gentle blue sky.

Brother Inchmahome considered Clair-de-Lune's statement gravely. If she had not been looking at him so earnestly, he might have laughed. But before he could make any response, Clair-de-Lune continued:

Inside I am wicked, I know. If I open my mouth, will I not be letting this wickedness out?

Now Brother Inchmahome was angry.

"Who told you you were wicked?" he said.

Clair-de-Lune looked at him timidly. She knew he was not angry with her, but she was a little frightened anyway. And she did not know how to answer him.

For no one needed to tell her. It was, surely—what was that word?—self-evident!

Self-evident, she said earnestly; and when she spoke, Brother Inchmahome almost mistook her voice for that of a seagull calling sadly from the rocks below.

"Self-evident?" he repeated, and his brow wrinkled in concentration as he tried to understand her. "It is not self-evident to me. You must be patient and explain to me. What is this wickedness you speak of?"

Clair-de-Lune's face was very serious.

Selfish, she said in that seagull voice.

Ungrateful, she added after a moment.

Cowardly, she said after another.

She was trying to explain to him about the heroic dancers in her grandmother's books, and how she was everything—selfish! ungrateful! cowardly!—they were not. She was trying to explain to him about her perfect mother, and about how terrible it was to have her mother's talent (as she was told she had) without her mother's nobility of spirit.

For Clair-de-Lune knew that she would never have the courage to give up her life for The Dance. The trouble was, too many things were more important to her. She had known for a long time that she would give up dancing if only she could speak. Now she knew that if she had to choose between Bonaventure or Brother Inchmahome and dancing, she would choose her friends. Now they, too, were more precious to her.

But how could she explain to him what a dreadful thing this was? To a dancer, she knew, nothing could be more important than The Dance. Nothing.

A *bad dancer*, she said in a soft, sad, seagull voice.

Then she looked at him and sighed hugely, with a kind of exhaustion. For there was other wickedness, she knew: caverns and dark valleys and sea bottoms of it, mysterious, inside her. She did not trust herself. She felt like a box that no one had opened. If she was careful and kept herself closed, perhaps she would do no harm.

But if she was opened?

Caverns! she said miserably. *Dark valleys! Sea bottoms!*

"Clair-de-Lune," said Brother Inchmahome.

And Clair-de-Lune looked up at him, startled. For she heard a new note in his voice, and this note had interrupted her sad thoughts. Now she forgot them and sat looking at him in wonder.

"Clair-de-Lune," said Brother Inchmahome—and his eyes were so kind and calm and serious, his voice so warm and gentle and certain—"you are not wicked. Inside, you are filled with goodness. Mountains and valleys, seas and deserts, vast skies and mysterious sea bottoms of goodness! We can all do wrong . . . sometimes great wrong. And there are times when we need to know what not to say. But you were given a soul— and you were given a voice. To speak—to tell the truth about yourself, what you think and feel—is not wrong. And no wickedness can escape in this way."

Clair-de-Lune gazed at him.

None at all? she said with her eyes.

Brother Inchmahome shook his head firmly.

"None at all," he said.

Clair-de-Lune stared down at the grass, her face tense with thought. What an astonishing man he was! Could what he was saying be true? *But,* she began, *but—*

"But now," said Brother Inchmahome, "I must give you another task. Those you have told me are not the only reasons you cannot speak, Clair-de-Lune. There are still more. For tomorrow, think of another."

A Few Good Mice

In a surprisingly comfortable—though often rather noisy—cavity behind the skirting board in a shadowy corner of the print shop where Bonaventure had had his posters copied, Leonard, the mouse who ran the underground printing press, was having a discussion with his wife.

"He's a good fellow, this Bonaventure—quite admirable, really. I mean, I don't see much in this dancing business of his myself, but every mouse should have a dream—like you and me, my dear, with the *Collected Works of Shakespeare for Mice*—and I admire his energy and persistence. A pity more mice aren't like him. But as for Juliet . . ."

"As for Juliet . . . ," said his wife.

"She's very young," said Leonard.

"Indeed," said his wife.

"And ballet dancing is by no means vital to her education—a mouse with proofreading talents like hers."

"By no means," agreed his wife.

"And," said Leonard in summary, "there is a Cat in that building."

"Enough said," his wife returned decisively.

"I think we must say no," said Leonard. "Will you call her in, Virginia?"

"Juliet, my dear?" called Virginia.

And Juliet appeared from around the corner, her whiskers twitching with expectation. She was a small, gray mouse, scarcely more than a pup, with large, expressive eyes and an unusually long and graceful tail.

"Yes, Mama?"

"Your father has something to tell you, my dear."

Juliet turned toward him hopefully.

"Juliet," began Leonard, "your mother and I have decided not to allow you to go to dancing lessons with Monsieur Bonaventure."

"Oh," said Juliet in a small voice.

"You are very young," continued her father, "and there is a Cat in that building. Your mother and I grew up with Cats, but you have never yet had to deal with one. There has fortunately never been a Cat in the print shop. We don't believe it would be wise to expose one so young and so inexperienced to such danger for the sake of merely learning to twiddle about on her toes. Don't be disappointed. There will, no doubt, be other op-portunities. And you have plenty to look forward to, you know. I may even let you proofread *Henry VI Part Three*, if you promise to be very careful."

But there would be no other opportunities to learn ballet,

and Juliet knew it. She brushed a tear away from her fur, murmured, "Yes, Papa," and went back to the hole around the corner that she used as her bedroom.

She had kept one of Bonaventure's posters and had tacked it up on the wall behind the warm, soft nest of clothing scraps, feathers, shredded newspaper, and fluff that was her bed. She looked up at it now through eyes filled with tears, and Bonaventure's precise calligraphy, which had seemed to promise a new life to her, swam into abstraction.

How Juliet had longed to learn to dance! Hearing about Bonaventure's dancing school had been the most exciting thing that had ever happened to her.

And now she was more disappointed than she had ever been in her life.

She had never really felt like she belonged in the printing business, noble though it was. Juliet loved beauty and romance, but her parents, though kind, only valued the intellect. They wanted mice to be informed, stimulated, and well-read, and had dedicated their lives to this. Juliet, though she was barely past puphood, did not so much want to read Shakespeare as to dance him.

But she was a gentle, stoic little mouse who respected her parents. They were eminently respectable mice. So she did not cry—although the tears swam in her eyes and her throat ached and ached. She just sat on her bed, cuddled her softest bit of fluff, and tried to find a way of thinking about it that would make it easier to bear.

Perhaps, she thought, *if I were to become a pupil, it would* somehow prevent some other mouse from joining the class who needed to more than me. Perhaps, if I knew all, I would know that this is for the best.

But, being intellectuals, Leonard and Virginia were still discussing their decision. One of their peculiarities as parents was that they were generally able to find as many arguments in favor of a proposition as they could find against it.

"She was very disappointed, wasn't she?" said Leonard to his wife.

"I did not realize how much it meant to her," admitted Virginia.

"Funny, the things she takes a fancy to! Oh, well, each to her own, I suppose."

"You know, Leonard, Cats are a fact of life."

"One of the most basic!" agreed Leonard.

"And she will have to learn how to deal with them eventually."

"That's true. She needs to learn caution. And to think on her feet."

"And she's never been what you would call *foolhardy*."

"No, indeed."

"In fact, she is careful to a fault. Hence her talent as a proofreader."

They were both silent for a moment.

"What say I take her over there, and we have a practice run?" said Leonard. "If I think she can do it, perhaps we might allow her after all."

"Just what I was thinking," said Virginia decisively. "Juliet?"

Juliet was a little surprised. She blew her nose, wiped her eyes, and crept back round the corner.

"Yes, Mama?"

"Your father has something to tell you, my dear."

Juliet turned to him inquiringly.

"Fetch your bonnet, my dear. I'm going to take you over to the dancing school."

"But—" faltered Juliet. "Why—"

"Never you mind. We shall see. Hurry up, my dear!"

Juliet's eyes grew wide with surprise and delight.

"Oh, thank you, Papa! Thank you, thank you, thank you!"

"Don't thank me yet. You must promise me to keep your eyes and ears open at all times."

"Especially when emerging from some place of protection," said her mother.

"And to remember your nose."

"A good nose is a mouse's best friend," said her mother.

"You must not daydream, or allow yourself to be distracted by anything."

"No matter how interesting," her mother put in.

"Whenever you are outside a place of safety, you must always be thinking about Cats."

"Only Cats. Nothing else."

"You must go straight there."

"And straight back!"

"Don't dawdle to look at anything."

"And never, ever go exploring. . . ."

Nevertheless, by that afternoon, Juliet had become Bonaventure's third pupil.

⊚ ⊚ ⊚

Scenes like this were taking place all over the mouse community. Scenes similar and yet different—as different as each of the mice and their circumstances.

There was the mouse from the cobbler's, who had been born in a ballet shoe and always felt that her destiny was somehow linked to The Dance. There was the mouse who lived at the Duke of Wellington (a public house), who had become so adept at entertaining his friends by dancing to the popular songs played by the piano player during the nightly sing-alongs that he had begun to think about dancing professionally. There was the sad mouse, who spent her long days concealed within a sunny window box staring out on the street below, and who desperately needed some new pursuit that might lift her spirits. And the happy mouse who could not sleep at night for pure joy, and who, having not yet found an adequate means of expression, hoped dancing might just be the thing. And then there was the mouse from the dressmaker's, who just wanted to be able to wear a *tutu*.

As Bonaventure worked in his mouse hole, planning his first class, a merry little breeze was springing up in the street outside.

It teased at, played with, and finally snatched up one of his posters—one that, a little hastily put up, had been flapping on its wall—and took it on a long, though fitful, journey.

For a little while it lay on the footpath, being walked over by people who, if they had noticed it at all, would have thought it was just a scrap of paper.

Then the breeze whisked it along one street, then another,

then died down and left it overnight in the gutter. But the next morning that merry little breeze became a wind that would not take no for an answer, and it blew the little poster—along with a lot of dust and leaves and twigs and other things too small to resist—up and over rooftops and chimneys and into a little town a few miles distant in the countryside on the outskirts of the city, where the day was as still as a lake of glass.

And there it was seen by a mouse who had dreamed all his life of dancing.

This mouse had fur like black silk and a soul so beautiful, so vulnerable, and so sweet that he was loved by all who knew him.

The journey to the city would be long and dangerous, he knew. But he packed his few belongings, said goodbye to all his friends, and set out that evening.

Bonaventure's school had not even started yet. But already it was changing the world.

Clair-de-Lune Changes Her Mind

One morning—so early that it was still as dark as night—Bonaventure crept out of his mouse hole (checking carefully left and right and all around first, for danger), across the floorboards of Monsieur Dupoint's classroom, under the double doors, and out onto the landing. He was carrying something under his arm—something about the size of the tiny scroll you find in a Christmas bonbon.

Once out on the landing, he unrolled it and pinned it onto the wall, centered directly below the stern sign that announced, as you'll remember:

**MONSIEUR DUPOINT'S SELECT
DANCING ACADEMY
FOR THE CHILDREN OF ARTISTES
WHO ASPIRE TO ENTER
THEIR PARENTS' PROFESSION**

Then he stood back to survey the effect.

He sighed with satisfaction.

Later that same morning, as Clair-de-Lune was about to go home to the attic after her visit with Brother Inchmahome, Bonaventure said to her:

"Mademoiselle Clair-de-Lune, I wonder if you would consider accompanying me downstairs for a—let us say extracurricular—visit to your esteemed place of study. There is something I would like to show you."

Clair-de-Lune followed politely. When they reached the floor, so quiet and still and empty at this early hour, and Bonaventure suddenly stopped short in front of the doors, looking proud and bashful at the same time, she was for a moment quite mystified. What was it he wanted her to see? Then it dawned on her that she would have to look for something at Bonaventure's eye level, and so she sank down onto her stomach and, lying full length on the floorboards, peered in the direction of his gaze.

Then she saw it, in tiny letters on a tiny poster not much more than an inch above the floor:

BONAVENTURE'S SELECT SCHOOL
FOR DANCER MICE
Inquire at mouse hole within

"An elegant sign, is it not?" said Bonaventure, peering anxiously into her face (only inches from his), partly bursting with pride, partly apprehensive in case she might not like it.

Clair-de-Lune nodded vigorously.

Bonaventure beamed. His whiskers stood out straight as steel and his black eyes shone. "Few people," he remarked, "appreciate the skill mice have attained in calligraphy!

"Will you permit me to show you inside?" he added, and disappeared immediately under the doors. Clair-de-Lune jumped up carefully, pushed them open a little, and squeezed through. (There was no lock on the doors of the school, as there was nothing inside it to steal—except perhaps the piano, but then you could never have got that down the stairs.) Bonaventure had already disappeared into his mouse hole. Again, Clair-de-Lune followed, lay down on her stomach, and peered inside. What she saw took her breath away.

The tiny dancing studio! The *barre*, at mouse-arm level— made of toothpicks! The mirrors! The curtained-off dressing rooms! And the pictures—the little pictures—of Arabella Moncrief and Myra Livingstone and Pierre-Nicolas Roulette!

Clair-de-Lune sighed—a long, delighted, astonished sigh. She had never seen anything so perfect in all her life.

"You think it is a good, professional-looking studio?" Bonaventure asked her anxiously.

And again Clair-de-Lune nodded vigorously. How could she reassure him? Awkwardly—for she was flat on her stomach with her cheek resting on the floorboards—she shifted position, kissed her hand, and blew the kiss into the studio. *Bellissimo!* she meant to say.

Bonaventure understood.

"I am profoundly flattered, mademoiselle," he said. "And now I must ask . . ." He drew himself up formally. "Our first meeting will be on Sunday. I would be so honored if you would attend! Moreover, will you, mademoiselle, be the patron of the school—and of the company, when it is formed?"

Clair-de-Lune was deeply touched. She blushed and sat up,

and Bonaventure hurried out of the mouse hole in order to see her answer.

Clair-de-Lune opened her hands as if to express that there was nothing in them—that she did not deserve such an honor. But then she clasped them over her heart and bowed her head.

"Oh, thank you, mademoiselle! Thank you! What a *coup* this is for my as yet emerging school!"

It was time for Clair-de-Lune to go, otherwise she would never be back in time for class—and in any case her grandmother would be worried. But just as she rose to leave, something caught her eye.

She leaned closer to the wall, just above the end of the *barre*.

It was a small drawing in chalk, a stick figure: a thin, ugly little girl dancing with her nose in the air. Below it, someone had written in chalk: *Clair-de-Lune is a snob*.

This was what they had been doing. This was what they had been laughing at. This was what they had called her over to see.

Mrs. Costello's Minette was sitting at the bottom of the stairs, just waiting, a black shadow against the wood, as Clair-de-Lune came out onto the landing. But when the door clattered behind her—for in her distraction Clair-de-Lune forgot to close it carefully—the cat took fright and disappeared.

Clair-de-Lune's grandmother was rather pleased when Clair-de-Lune couldn't eat her breakfast. That was one less meal to worry about—she could have it for her lunch—and in any case Clair-de-Lune's grandmother cherished the hope that one day

Clair-de-Lune, like Eleanor Wood, might attain that state of perfection among dancers where she would not find it necessary to eat at all. In fact, she was somewhat ashamed that their poverty posed any problem. For real dancers, she felt, it shouldn't have: real dancers wouldn't need to eat.

When Clair-de-Lune had changed into her practice frock and kissed her grandmother, she left the attic again to go to her morning class. But as she got closer and closer to the school, she walked more and more slowly down the stairs.

Finally, she stopped altogether, paused, and sat down on a step. Minette was dozing in the small patch of sun that shone dustily through the window nearby, but Clair-de-Lune was too anxious to pat her.

It would be hard to go to class today.

Of course, she had already known that none of the other girls liked her. And she knew why, too: it was because she could not speak and because they thought she was not speaking on purpose; it was because her mother was La Lune and she, Clair-de-Lune, was Monsieur Dupoint's pet; and it was also because her fair hair and her thinness and her pale little face made her seem somehow rarefied, regal, just as her silence and dreaminess implied that she was lost in thoughts too elevated to share. From a distance, she was easy to dislike. She knew that.

But somehow the drawing and the caption underneath it had changed things, or at least her understanding of them. Before, she had hoped that speaking would solve all this: if she could speak, she would be able to explain herself, show herself, and when she had done so they would not dislike her anymore. She had thought that not speaking was a barrier. Now, because she had seen the drawing and the caption, she had somehow felt the full force of their dislike of her, and saw that she was in a danger she had not understood before. And when you are in danger, you do not expose yourself further.

For the first time she realized that not being able to speak was a kind of protection.

It was painful to be disliked for who she was, and how she looked, and other things she could not help. It was painful to be disliked because she was misunderstood. But to be disliked for her real self—for the Clair-de-Lune who would speak out of her heart, if that heart had a voice—ah! that would be unbearable.

She had changed her mind. She must not learn to speak. She would have to tell Brother Inchmahome tomorrow.

She thought he would be disappointed, and this hurt her, but she pushed the thought aside. She could not worry about that now. She had to go to class.

But what was she to do about her dancing?

Clair-de-Lune hid her face in her hands, thinking, thinking.

Of course, dancing was the problem, or a large part of it. They did not like her because she danced too well. And that, of course, was why she was Monsieur Dupoint's pet. She could not change her mother. She could not change her looks. But she could, she supposed, dance badly.

But if she danced badly, she would be in trouble with Monsieur Dupoint, and then he would say something, and then they would all laugh and be glad.

And if she danced badly, she would be betraying her mother and her grandmother and her Sacred Art.

What to do? What to do?

If she didn't move now, she would be late.

Clair-de-Lune forced herself to stand and continue down the stairs. Each step took new strength; she felt as if she were walking through molasses. She got down to the last flight of steps; she reached the landing outside the school. The usual gaggle of girls was milling round the door. She passed through them, her face pale and calm, though her stomach ached with fear and misery.

"Snob," Milly whispered, and the rest burst into giggles.

Then, mercifully, Monsieur Dupoint called the class to order, and they all took their places.

But Clair-de-Lune could not decide how to dance. In an erratic sort of way, she tried to dance not too well and not too badly. But it was not as easy as she'd thought. Dancing well came almost instinctively to her. And it is not easy to go against instinct.

Monsieur Dupoint noticed that there was something very odd about Clair-de-Lune's dancing that morning. But this time, wisely, he said nothing.

It Is Better to Have Loved and Lost

I have decided, said Clair-de-Lune very sadly the next morning to Brother Inchmahome, *that it is best, after all, for me not to learn to speak. I am sorry, Brother Inchmahome, for having put you to all this trouble. But there it is.*

Brother Inchmahome sat up on his heels. He had been contemplating the tiny, rock-colored crabs that lived in one particular rock pool at the base of the cliff below the monastery. Now he contemplated Clair-de-Lune.

"Clair-de-Lune!" he said mildly. "But why?"

That morning he had taken them out through the back garden and showed them an extraordinary thing. In that garden on the cliff, with its sheer drop to the sea, there was what looked like a well, surrounded by wildflowers. But it wasn't a well. It was the beginning of a spiral staircase, cut downward into the rock!

"This is how the brothers get to the beach," he had said, and scooped up Bonaventure and began the descent.

But Clair-de-Lune had hesitated.

Brother Inchmahome had discerned already that Clair-de-Lune was sad this morning. Now he saw that she was afraid.

Clair-de-Lune was no coward. Dancers have to be brave; it is part of their discipline. Clair-de-Lune had done classes during which Monsieur Dupoint had elevated her high into the air, holding her with only one hand, and then swung her back down so that she soared through the air like a feeding swallow, grazing the floor in an upswinging arc.

But so little of Clair-de-Lune's life had been spent outside! Thus, all her bravery was indoor bravery. And so she knew the bravery required of dancers, and the bravery you needed when you lie awake at night, in the dark, alone with your imagination and your fears. She knew the bravery it took to bear being confined, buried among roofs and stairways and ceilings, with no way out, and the bravery she needed to endure the fear of her grandmother's displeasure. And, of course, she knew just how much bravery was required to go into a room in which, she felt, almost everyone disliked her.

But, although she longed for them, she knew nothing of cliffs and climbing and beaches. She could not judge whether this was a safe thing to do.

"You need not come down if you do not wish, Clair-de-Lune," said Brother Inchmahome. He had paused on the stairway and was looking up at her from a few steps down into the well, his head to one side. "But the stairway is quite safe. Why, even Brother Juniper, who cooks for us, comes down here, and he is not light on his feet. If a bear like that can manage these stairs, I'm sure that you—a dancer—will have no trouble. And the beach is very beautiful." He glanced up at her again—a quick, interested, amused glance, as if wondering what she was going to do. Then, with Bonaventure riding on his shoulder, he continued down the stairs.

Clair-de-Lune hesitated for a moment longer.

Then, holding carefully on to the ground around the opening, she climbed down the first few stairs. Now her hands, holding on to the grass, were at waist level. She climbed down a few more. Now her hands were level with her eyes. The steps were large and very sturdy. Around them was a wall of rock. Clair-de-Lune let go and kept walking slowly down the stairs. She was not sure whether she liked the feeling or not. She did not feel as if she was going to fall, and yet there was something alarming about traveling so deep down through solid rock. She looked up. The sky was clearly visible, a circle of blue above. She could see birds flying past. As she continued down farther into the cave, round and round and down and down, the light became dimmer, and the sky disappeared. But just as she thought it was going to get truly dark, she began to perceive a light, a gray light like dawn, coming not from above but from below. A few more steps and the light was stronger. She could hear a murmuring and a rushing, and the calls of seagulls. Then suddenly the stairway led into the open air, and she was climbing down the last stretch of stairs, down the base of the cliff with the sea all around her, to the beach, which was part sand and part rock. All at once the steps disappeared into the sand.

Brother Inchmahome was waiting for her on the beach, his brown robes and his dark hair stirring in the gentle morning sea breeze.

"The sea! The sea!" Bonaventure was squeaking from the monk's shoulder (and Brother Inchmahome put his hand up quickly to support him in case, in his excitement, he should fall). "Ah, this takes me back to the days of my earliest youth! My happy childhood with my nine brothers and sisters! How peacefully we slept in our seashell, with the sound of my mother's mouse lullabies in our happy ears! And with what gusto we played on the beach outside the fisherman's cottage! Marmaduke, Bartholomew, Demetrius, Oscar, Lavinia, Francesca, Anastasia, Miriam, and Joan—dear little Joan . . . Where are they all now, I wonder? No doubt they have forged their separate careers. And Mother—dear Mother! I must go back to see her when I have started the company. How surprised she will be! 'You see, Mother,' I will say, 'there is more to life than Limitations!' "

But Clair-de-Lune was not listening.

She was too shocked.

To be suddenly so close to something so completely outside . . .

For there is nothing more open, more outside, than the sea. The freedom of it! The vastness of it! Her head spun. She sat down suddenly on a nearby rock and simply stared.

And yet, she thought, *I am still inside the house. How surprising life is.*

"What has made you change your mind?" pressed Brother Inchmahome gently.

Clair-de-Lune looked deeply into the rock pool. The sand-colored crabs were hard to see. Whenever you became aware of one, it seemed at first not as if a sand-colored crab was moving about in the water, but as if some of the sand had got up and walked.

I know now that speaking is dangerous, she said in the baby-bird voice that only Brother Inchmahome could understand. *If I do not speak, no one will ever really be able to dislike me, because no one will ever really know me. If I do speak, then it will be possible for people to dislike not just the person they think I am, but the person I am.*

Brother Inchmahome, I do not want to be disliked. I would rather be alone.

Brother Inchmahome looked at her through eyes as gray as a dawn sky and as clear as water.

"I see," he said.

And then he thought for what seemed a very long time.

And the gentle waves scurried up the beach and then back down into the sea like waves of mice; and the blue morning sky grew bluer, and the sun became warmer on their backs; and the seagulls coasted stiffly like paper-and-wood kites in the breeze and made their harsh, lonely remarks. And Brother Inchmahome got up quietly and came to sit beside her on her rock.

"But," he said at last, and his face was very serious, and it seemed to her indeed that the deep thoughts of his heart were written there in its gravity and sweetness, "if you do not speak, no one will ever really be able to like you, either. It is as you say. No one can truly like, or dislike, what they do not know. I suppose it is a question of whether you think the gamble worthwhile, knowing you may lose. But it is a noble gamble,

Clair-de-Lune, a valiant gamble! I think it is better to have loved and lost, as Tennyson has put it, than never to have loved at all, don't you?" Here Brother Inchmahome paused, his eyes distant and dreamy. "But that," he resumed after a moment, "is something you must decide for yourself.

"And Clair-de-Lune," he added, "when you're deciding"—and here his eyes shone with humor—"do not forget that every person you have spoken to so far has liked you. I call that an excellent batting average!"

Clair-de-Lune could not help but smile at that, for of course she had spoken only to Brother Inchmahome so far.

"But I also have a question to ask you," he continued. "Does a seed in the earth ask itself whether anyone is going to like it before it sprouts and pushes itself up through the soil and grows until it becomes a flower? And should it?"

Clair-de-Lune stared into the rock pool, thinking. She thought of the girls in her class, and of how much they disliked her. She saw again the chalk drawing—*Am I as ugly in their eyes as the little chalk dancer?* she thought—and the caption beneath it. She heard the whisper, "Snob!" Then her eyes filled with tears, for she had thought of something else.

Oh, Brother Inchmahome, she said in the voice of a baby bird, weeping, *if one speaks, it becomes possible to hurt someone! If I speak and hurt someone—what then?*

Brother Inchmahome turned his kind face toward her once more and said with great seriousness:

"But through speech, also, it is possible to heal someone, Clair-de-Lune. If you never speak, you will never harm through speech, it is true. But if you never speak, you will never be able to help through speech, either."

Clair-de-Lune gazed at him in surprise. Would she—Clair-de-Lune, of all people—ever be able to help anyone?

"Clair-de-Lune," said Brother Inchmahome, "have you decided to continue your lessons?"

Clair-de-Lune looked at him solemnly and then, slowly, nodded.

"May I give you yet another task, then? There are still more reasons, I think, why you cannot speak. Tomorrow, tell me another."

Clair-de-Lune Hears Something Subversive in Church

On Sundays, Clair-de-Lune did not dance. On Sundays, Clair-de-Lune went to church. On this particular Sunday, something happened that Clair-de-Lune's grandmother had worried about, in a vague, back-of-the-mind kind of way, for years. Clair-de-Lune heard something subversive in church.

That morning, Clair-de-Lune dressed, as usual, in the dress—her best—that she always wore to church. All of Clair-de-Lune's clothes were cut down from dresses of her mother's. La Lune had had a good many clothes in the days of her celebrity, and Clair-de-Lune's grandmother had made them last. She had never had to buy anything new for Clair-de-Lune since her babyhood. And she was hoping that the clothes—which she kept carefully packed away in a trunk in the attic—would last Clair-de-Lune until she was sixteen or so and able to earn some money as a dancer. Thus Clair-de-Lune was always decently—if at times slightly oddly—attired.

Clair-de-Lune's white practice dress was cut down from a nightgown of her mother's. Her gray and white striped day gown with its pink sash had been cut down from a similar day gown La Lune had worn. There were clothes—evening gowns and so forth—that little use could be made of, owing to the grandness of their material. Clair-de-Lune's grandmother kept them carefully, for if ever their poverty became desperate, the gowns could be sold, to keep them going a little longer. She had not, however, judged their need sufficient so far.

Clair-de-Lune had always liked wearing her mother's clothes, for it made her mother seem closer, not so far away. She admired her mother so much that it was impossible for her to feel worthy to be her daughter. But when she remembered that she was wearing her clothes, she felt a bond with her, as if she were still present—even, a little, as if the two of them were somehow alike. Curiously, in Clair-de-Lune's head, it was almost as if La Lune were two people—the Perfect Dancer of the press clippings and her grandmother's stories, and the woman who had worn clothes that, even many years after her death, could still be cut down to keep her daughter warm.

There was one dress in which Clair-de-Lune felt closer to her mother than any other. This was the dress she wore to church.

It was violet, this dress, with an emerald-green sash and a white lace collar and cuffs. She had a matching violet bonnet lined with white lace, with a green ribbon to tie under her chin, and little emerald-green silk gloves. It was, of course, her best dress, and not, perhaps, to everyone's taste. But when she wore it, Clair-de-Lune felt as though she were living in the heart of a posy of violets—and as if her mother were living there with her.

The dress had indeed been her mother's favorite. But Clair-de-Lune's grandmother had never told her so.

On this particular Sunday morning, as Clair-de-Lune was tying the ribbon of her bonnet and looking at herself in the ancient, greenish glass of the mirror she shared with her grandmother, she had a sudden, vivid thought.

Her mother must once have been a girl of just Clair-de-Lune's age. La Lune must once have been twelve years old.

She was used to conceiving of her mother only as a grownup dancer, for that, after all, was the only part of La Lune's life her grandmother ever spoke of. This was not the first time Clair-de-Lune had thought of her mother as a child. But somehow it had never before come into her mind quite so sharply.

Had she been the same height as Clair-de-Lune—or perhaps taller?

Had her skin been as pale—or paler?

Did she have a friend as good as Bonaventure or Brother Inchmahome?

But then Clair-de-Lune heard that voice again, the voice muffled by layers and layers of she did not know what, trying to tell her something. She almost stopped it, as usual, by thinking immediately of something else.

But she was feeling so strong today, so questioning and adventurous, that she paused, still staring into the mirror, and carefully brought herself back.

What was it, this noise, this voice that frightened her so much? Why was it so frightening? What was it trying to say?

And for a moment, her heart thumping, she thought she began to hear something that may have been words.

But then her grandmother spoke to her sharply.

"Clair-de-Lune! You know that I cannot abide vanity! Stop that mirror gazing immediately, or you will be late to church!"

So, coming to herself with a little start, and hurrying to fetch her lavender-scented white lace handkerchief and a coin for the collection, Clair-de-Lune dutifully kissed her grandmother and set off down the stairs.

As usual, she had already passed the floor that contained the stone door to the monastery before she remembered to look for it, and so was confused yet again about where it actually was. When she got to Monsieur Dupoint's floor, the third, she found Bonaventure waiting for her, his whiskery nose peeking out from under the door into the ballet school.

"That Cat has been about—I can smell her," he explained, emerging cautiously. "Good morning, Mademoiselle Clair-de-Lune!" he went on. "I thought I might have missed you. I wonder if you would allow me to accompany you to Divine Service this morning. I am, in truth," he added, wringing his paws, "too nervous to stay home."

For, of course, the great day had come. Today, at last, was the opening day of Bonaventure's school.

Clair-de-Lune picked him up carefully. He was trembling. Cradling him in her hands, she brought him up close to her face and rubbed her cheek softly against his fur. She felt his cold little whiskered nose trembling against her skin. Then, very gently, she kissed him on the top of his tiny head.

"Support much appreciated, I'm sure," said Bonaventure.

Clair-de-Lune slipped the mouse carefully into the pocket of her skirt. There he could travel comfortably with his nose poking out into the fresh air. Then she continued down the stairs.

The street outside was empty and quiet, for there was no market on Sundays. The small jagged oblong of sky above them was blue, but the street was in shadow and felt cool and damp, for until the middle of the day no sunlight could manage to shine its way past the tall, crammed buildings. The church, St. Mary's, stood at the end of the street, its side door facing them. Clair-de-Lune set out toward it. But she had not gone three steps before the church bells began to ring, calling across the red-brown rooftops with a voice of freedom.

Clair-de-Lune stood still for a moment and closed her eyes. She loved the sound of church bells. They seemed so unafraid. Then she hurried, holding Bonaventure steady in her hand, along the empty street, up the steps, and into the church.

In her usual place in the second back pew, in the shadow of a stone pillar that looked like a tree trunk, Clair-de-Lune sat with her green-silk-gloved hands folded neatly on her violet skirt, Bonaventure peering out from between her fingers.

But as Clair-de-Lune and Bonaventure sat waiting for Matins to begin, mice—one here, one there—all over the theater district were getting ready for their first ballet class.

Margot and Rudolph, having arranged to meet early in a window box full of flowers that belonged to a lady who lived not far from Clair-de-Lune's building, were canoodling, in the manner of engaged couples.

"Are you looking forward to our first dancing lesson?" whispered Margot tenderly into Rudolph's ear.

Rudolph nibbled affectionately at the pink ribbon around Margot's neck.

"Not really," he sighed blissfully. They were so very much in love.

At the print shop, Leonard had been reminding Juliet all morning about the fact that Bonaventure's building had a Cat and about how careful and sensible she would need to be. Juliet was trying to do a little proofreading on *Henry VI Part Three* before she left, but she was too excited to concentrate.

The mouse from the cobbler's, who had been putting a crumb or two aside every day, was eating a particularly good, though rather stale, breakfast, for she was determined not to feel faint during the class. The mouse from the Duke of Wellington, who always had a good breakfast, was practicing some of his better steps, in case he should be asked for a demonstration. The sad mouse had already started for the building—her sadness made her walk so slowly that she was afraid of being late. And the happy mouse was visiting a sick friend who lived on the way. The mouse from the dressmaker's was trying to decide what to wear.

And the mouse with the fur like black silk and the beautiful soul was still journeying through the countryside, long days yet from his destination.

Meanwhile, back at the church, Clair-de-Lune was picking out for herself all the people she knew in the congregation. Of course, she could only see the backs of their heads. But they were not so hard to recognize. There was Mrs. Costello, wearing her old-fashioned Sunday bonnet, which trembled a little as she thought her flustered thoughts. There was Mr. Kirk, the actor, with his long, rather disheveled gray-streaked dark hair, his head thrown back defiantly, easy to pick out because he was so tall. There was Miss Blossom, the singing teacher, who even when sitting seemed to hold herself in a fully supported kind of way, as if her chest were permanently inflated like a balloon. Clair-de-Lune thought, *They don't know I'm here, because I always sit at the back and sneak out before them. What if I were to wait and smile at them as they passed? Would they smile back?*

Would I dare try it?

She was so distracted by this astonishing thought that when the organ began to crash its way splendidly through hymn number 492 she almost cried out with fright. But she collected herself, slipped Bonaventure back into her pocket, stood with the rest of the congregation, and mouthed dutifully through the verses in her hymn book. When the hymn had been sung as loudly as possible, their vicar, the Reverend Dr. Balthazar Misslethwaite, said, "Let us pray!" and they all knelt while he led them through a long and sonorous prayer.

Then it was time for the first lesson.

A man walked up to the lectern, paused for a moment, told the congregation where the lesson was taken from—

And read aloud a passage that would change Clair-de-Lune's life.

"*If I speak,*" he read, "*in the tongues of men and of angels, and have not love, I am but a sounding gong or a tinkling cymbal. . . .*"

Slowly, Clair-de-Lune sat up and leaned forward. She had

been so startled by the first sentence that she had already missed several of the following ones. Her mind raced to catch up. But among the strange, beautiful words, all she really heard was:

Love . . .

Love . . .

Love . . .

And yet, she knew what was being said. The passage was saying that there was nothing more important than love. Nothing.

The service continued, but Clair-de-Lune was not following it anymore. The congregation prayed and sang, there was a sermon and a collection, the choir sang something, they were blessed and sent tumbling out into the daylight again. But through it all she could only think, *Nothing is more important than love. Nothing. Therefore* . . .

Love is more important than The Dance.

Could this be true?

Clair-de-Lune stood in her pew, no longer really remembering where she was. Vaguely, she noticed the very tall Mr. Kirk shuffling past on his way out; she smiled at him absentmindedly—a crooked little smile, for she was somewhat out of practice—and, raising his eyebrows, he grinned back with a grin that transformed his face.

She had never heard it said before, that anything was more important than The Dance. She had thought that The Dance was the most important thing. She had thought that she was wrong to want something more than dancing. Could it be that she had been right?

Miss Blossom passed by. Clair-de-Lune smiled crookedly. Miss Blossom opened her mouth with surprise—and then winked at her with a jolly sort of camaraderie.

But that would mean that her grandmother was wrong! At the very least, it was beginning to look as if the Church disagreed with her grandmother. This was a possibility Clair-de-Lune had never considered before. She had always imagined the two of them to be in cahoots.

But worse still, it would mean that her mother was wrong, and that was something Clair-de-Lune could not bear. For to her mother, of course, dancing had been the most important thing in the world.

Clair-de-Lune stumbled out of church—shook the vicar's hand—almost bumped into Mrs. Costello—smiled in apology—received a flustered little smile in return—walked down the steps and hurried away, in turmoil.

Of course, it would also mean that love was more important even than speaking, thought Clair-de-Lune. *For if I speak in the tongues of men and of angels, but have not love, I am but a sounding gong or a tinkling cymbal. . . .*

Ah, but of course it was true!

For the first time, Clair-de-Lune understood that speaking was simply her way to love.

Thus it was, at last, that Clair-de-Lune heard the subversive thing in church that her grandmother had been fearing.

But the day was still young.

Bonaventure's First Class

"Of course, no one may show up. No one at all!"

Bonaventure laughed a tiny, tinkling bell of a mouse laugh. He was speaking very quickly, as he tended to do when nervous.

"I have had inquiries, enrollments even, but . . . Perhaps I have caused scandal by commencing on a Sunday. Dancing is, after all, work—and that of a most serious kind. But it seemed wise to gather for the first time on a day when the school would be empty of humans. And Brother Inchmahome approved. He said the Sabbath was made for man, not man for the Sabbath—and that it was not made for mice at all. You are coming, are you not, to observe the first class? That is, if there is a first class. My teaching career may be over before it has even begun. . . ."

He laughed again, a little hysterically, then grew abruptly serious.

"Oh, Mademoiselle Clair-de-Lune, do you think this is a terrible mistake? Do you think I can do it?"

Clair-de-Lune was walking up the stairs in a dream. *Love!* she thought. *Love!*

Of course you can do it, she said in her baby-bird voice.

But although Bonaventure could hear her, of course, he could not understand what she'd said.

Nevertheless, he was beginning to draw on his own not inconsiderable reserves of courage.

"Mademoiselle," he began slowly, with a little upward tilt of his tiny chin, "I am wrong to worry like this. For if there is only one pupil awaiting me—even if there is only one—I shall take it as a sign that I am meant to continue. In order to teach, I need but one pupil. And if I teach just one mouse to dance, my whole career will be worthwhile!

"Take, if you will, Brother Inchmahome. He is, after all, teaching only one child to speak. And that, mademoiselle, is the most worthwhile thing I have ever witnessed."

Clair-de-Lune could not help but kiss him for that. Then, just inside the door of Monsieur Dupoint's empty classroom, and with an extra little cuddle, she placed him gently down on the floor. He waved jauntily at her, drew himself up, and walked with perfect dignity and confidence into his mouse hole.

Then she heard a funny thing, a sound she could not at first recognize.

She tried to imagine what it might be.

Then she realized. It was the sound of many pairs of mouse hands, clapping.

Presently Bonaventure reappeared in the doorway of his classroom. His eyes were shining with emotion. He beckoned to her and went back inside. Clair-de-Lune lay down carefully on the floorboards, hoping not to damage her dress. When she looked into the mouse hole, a delightful sight met her eyes.

At the *barres* along the walls of Bonaventure's classroom stood not one but twenty-four dancer mice. Twenty-four pairs of bright black eyes met hers. Then twenty-four pairs of mice hands applauded again.

There was Margot, snow-white with her customary pink ribbon tied in a bow around her neck. There was Rudolph, pushing his spectacles back up his nose. There was Juliet, who had (you will be pleased to hear) arrived in one piece (although her parents were counting the minutes until she could be expected home) and who looked smaller and grayer and shyer than everyone else. And there, standing in one place or another along the *barres*, were the mice from the cobbler's and the Duke of Wellington, the sad mouse, the happy mouse, the mouse from the dressmaker's (who felt frustratedly that her ensemble was all wrong), and others.

But the mouse with fur like black silk and a beautiful soul was still on the road, traveling steadily toward his destination, a little hungry but full of hope.

"This," announced Bonaventure, "is our patron, the great dancer Mademoiselle Clair-de-Lune, who has magnanimously blessed us with her support and interest. She is here today to observe our first class. Now, *mesdemoiselles, messieurs—attention, s'il vous plaît!* We shall commence, of course, with *pliés!* First position—like so! Draw yourselves up—like so! Tails tucked under! Tummies pulled in! Heads erect! *And—*"

And so Bonaventure began his teaching career.

◎ ◎ ◎

111

Clair-de-Lune had been watching the mice's class for some twenty minutes when Monsieur Dupoint came in. She was so absorbed (for there can be hardly anything more delightful, it must be said, than watching a ballet class exclusively for mice) that she did not notice him until he was halfway across the room. The door clattered behind him. The mice stopped dancing.

Clair-de-Lune was dismayed. What was he doing here? It was Sunday! And what would he think she was doing? It was vital that she did not draw attention to the mice—she doubted she could make him understand, and there could be talk of traps and cats and who knew what else. But without a good reason, how could she explain her presence here on Sunday morning in his empty classroom? Not being able to talk would not help her here. What if he was to tell Grandmama?

Slowly, quietly, carefully, she moved away from the mouse hole and into the far corner.

Meanwhile, in the mouse hole, Bonaventure had realized what had happened, and in his class there was a brief flutter of uncertainty.

"She has gone!" exclaimed Margot. "Mademoiselle our patron observes us no longer!"

"Someone has come in," said Rudolph, putting his arm around Margot protectively. "Should we disperse?"

"No," said Bonaventure. Immediately there was silence. Every mouse eye was upon him, and as he stood there at the front of the class, his head held high, his dark eyes shining, he looked, thought Juliet, incomparably noble. "We must carry on. There will be many interferences, many distractions, many dangers. It is not easy to be a dancer mouse. For now, let us return to our *grands battements*. And . . ."

Clair-de-Lune sat very still in the corner. Monsieur Dupoint had not as yet noticed her. He had come in with another man—a *danseur* from the Company—presumably to snatch some extra rehearsal time, and was deep in conversation. It was sad to have to leave Bonaventure's class, but it would undoubtedly be better not to be seen. Clair-de-Lune thought that if she was very quiet and waited for a moment when they were both looking away, she could slip out the door without them seeing her. But every time she was ready to try, one of them would turn his head, and she would be forced to sink down again, out of sight.

"And was she as beautiful as they say?" said the *danseur*. He was warming up, doing *pliés* at the *barre*.

"Ah, *certainement*. Yes! More beautiful. She had a cloud of wild dark hair and a pale oval face. Her eyes—they were like stars! She had such life, such light, such warmth! To this day I find it hard to believe I will never see her again. But they wanted to make her choose, you see—they all wanted to make her choose. She couldn't be a dancer and a woman, oh no! She had to be either one or the other. And they left her in no doubt as to which would be the inferior choice. They couldn't see that the life and the light and the warmth of her dancing was fed by her love. That was the kind of dancer she was. . . ."

Suddenly Clair-de-Lune felt strange. She wanted to go, and yet something was tugging at her, urging her to stay. *Listen! Listen!* this thing said. *They are talking about . . . They are talking about . . .* But whom were they talking about?

113

"When you say *they*, whom do you mean? Who was forcing her to choose?"

"Oh, her mother—the old lady, you know—and the head of the Company of the day. She was very young—and gentle, despite her wildness. Part of her always wanted to please. The old lady was an extraordinary dancer, too—I remember her from my childhood, you know. But as a girl she had been disappointed in love. Dreadfully so, by all accounts. And so she wanted her daughter to keep away from men and love and marriage. However, the girl wouldn't—she couldn't. Then they told her that if she married him she'd be dropped from the Company."

"An idle threat, surely?"

"She believed it. She broke it off. But she died, onstage, within the year—and I swear to God, she died of a broken heart."

The *danseur* whistled and stopped still for a moment.

"And what became of him?" he asked softly.

"The man she loved? Oh, his heart was broken, too. He went away—made a new life for himself, in another country, I think—and was never heard of again. The old lady never even met him. I doubt he ever knew he had a child." Monsieur Dupoint paused. "I'm worried about the child. She is her mother all over again, but with hair as fair as moonlight! Every day she gets thinner . . . and now she can't seem to keep her mind on her dancing. The director has been talking to me about her, you know. They want to use her in the hundredth-birthday celebration. She's a born dancer, it's true. But I would rather her stop dancing than kill herself like her mother did."

They both turned suddenly toward the window as a strange bird with silver feathers soared past. But Clair-de-Lune did not hear their exclamations about it; in her shock and confusion, she had heard nothing about herself at all. She slipped suddenly and silently out the door, unobserved. Once on the landing, she sank down onto the floorboards, trembling.

So, said a still, quiet voice in her mind, beneath, behind, below her grief and astonishment, *love is more important than The Dance.*

My mother thought so, too.

"You're very late, child!" Clair-de-Lune's grandmother observed.

Clair-de-Lune was relieved that she had managed to get up the stairs at all. There were six flights between Monsieur Dupoint's floor and the attic, and when you are trembling, that is a long way. She was pale, but her grandmother did not notice. She couldn't eat her lunch, but her grandmother was only pleased.

As it was Sunday, Clair-de-Lune spent the afternoon working at her *petit point,* while her grandmother read aloud to her from the usual volumes. But Clair-de-Lune could not concentrate. For the first time, she thought, *Where are the stories of friendship and love? Are there none? Do writers not write about friendship or love?* Suddenly, without friendship, without love, the heroic sacrifices of the great dancers seemed empty.

Dancing is a cruel god, thought Clair-de-Lune. *But that is because it is not meant to be a god.*

Bonaventure's Vision

That night, as darkness fell, Bonaventure paced in his mouse hole.

From time to time, briefly, he would stop in the center of the room, staring intently into space. Then he would change direction, walk to the corner, and throw himself into his tiny chair.

And then he would gaze, unseeing, in front of him at the mouse-sized writing desk with the miniature crucifix and the tiny vase of artificial flowers, all of which had been a fortunate inheritance from a friend with access to a dollhouse (and of course the desk came in so handy for paperwork).

But then, almost immediately, he would leap up again and pace rapidly from one end of the room to the other. His black eyes shone. His whiskers stood out straight and as silver as steel.

When Clair-de-Lune had been forced to abandon her observation of Bonaventure's class, he had been disappointed, of course. But he had often read of great artists who had risen above personal difficulties—the death of a dear friend or relative, for example, on the night of a performance—not only to go on and perform, but to give the best performance of their lives. And so he had drawn upon his inner strength (and the good sense that told him that there would, in all likelihood, be other classes for Clair-de-Lune to observe) and carried on.

He had taken his class through their exercises at the *barre*, counting the time and hearing the music in his head. (He had not yet found a mouse pianist or a suitable instrument, but he was in negotiation with the mouse who lived in the organ at St. Mary's—a gifted musician, though quite deaf.) He had demonstrated each exercise and moved up and down the room, observing each student and pausing to correct the position of a leg, or the carriage of a paw. He had developed, for his students, his groundbreaking ideas about tails (an element never before taken into account in the teaching of classical ballet), which he felt ought to be draped neatly over the crook of one's right front paw when not in use, but used as a fifth limb in such heightened dramatic moments as the *pas de deux*.

Then he had brought them into the center and taught them *ports de bras*, and *pirouettes*, and *pas de chat*. He had even experimented a little with lifts. He had seen the expressions on his students' faces—of respect and dedication, and of passionate interest. And when at last he had taught them the *révérence* (for females) and the *salut* (for males); when at last, looking carefully out of the mouse hole first, they had departed, one by one, with a "*Merci*, Monsieur Bonaventure!"

and an *"Au revoir!"* Bonaventure had understood something—an astonishing, revolutionary thing—that had never been clear to him before.

What was it Brother Inchmahome had said?

Mice are the best dancers. One has only to see one move to know that. Mice dance with their whiskers. They dance with their tails. They spend their lives dancing. It is they who taught us. . . .

It was true. Humans had to learn to dance. Mice already knew.

"I must see the stars!" said Bonaventure rapturously, out loud. And he pulled his threadbare coat from the coat stand, strode back across the room, looked carefully out the door, and ventured into Monsieur Dupoint's empty classroom.

The window was at the opposite end. Bonaventure skipped along the skirting boards, then scaled the side of the cold stove and leaped onto the windowsill. Fortunately, the window was open a crack, and already the stars were twinkling in the sky. Bonaventure rested on the windowsill, stared up at the sky, and took a deep breath.

He was so excited, so elated, that he barely knew how to contain himself. He thought he might burst with happiness.

And if I do, he thought, *perhaps I will become one of the stars!* For Bonaventure had read a story in which just such an event had taken place.

He had dreamed of starting a dancing school. And there had been another dream—to start a company. But he had thought that a long way off.

Now, however, he knew that not only his first dream but also his second was within his grasp.

He had not expected his students to be dancers already.

Now that he knew they were, he saw that he already had his company! They were the four and twenty mice who had spent the afternoon in his mouse hole.

A company! A company of dancing mice!

Bonaventure gazed at the stars. The sky had darkened even as he had been sitting there, and more and more stars were appearing on its dark, fathomless backdrop. It was a stage—the sky was a stage! And as Bonaventure sat and dreamed, the stars swam together and became mice.

Mice! In exquisite costumes! Their tails draped elegantly over the crooks of their right paws as—the females on one side and the males on the other—they danced in formation, a delicate court dance. For—yes! (thought Bonaventure)—it was the age of chivalry, of mouse knights and mouse ladies, and all was courtesy and grace and nobility. But then (as Bonaventure gazed and dreamed) the court scene faded and the Mouse Prince stood on the battlements of the castle. He had run from the banquet, hearing the call of a strange wild creature, and as he stared into the sky above the castle he saw a magical bird— a bird with a heart of fire—fly overhead and disappear into the night. He must follow it!

Ah, but (of course, thought Bonaventure) in order to follow this quest he must leave his mouse lady behind, and he cannot even promise to return to her, for the quest may claim his life! Bonaventure saw a *pas de deux*: two mice dancing to express their love for one another, and their sadness at parting—the Mouse Prince's valor and nobility, his lady's generous sacrifice— their tails entwined. And then he saw the Mouse Prince setting out on his quest to follow the bird with the heart of fire. . . .

Bonaventure shivered. Suddenly, in the night air, he was cold. But his head was still full of stars. He leaped from the windowsill, climbed down the stove, and sped back along the skirting boards and into his mouse hole. He flew to the writing desk and lit the candle that stood on top of it, in front of the crucifix. Then he opened the top drawer. It was filled with discarded toffee papers, which Bonaventure had ironed flat with a tiny iron (constructed with some difficulty from a bottle top). In this way he had collected many sheets of mouse writing paper. Now he took one, shut the drawer, and settled impatiently at the desk to write.

The Prince's Quest

he scratched at the top of the toffee paper with a tiny quill, dipped in a hollowed-out orange pip filled with ink, and added below it:

A Ballet for Mice

And by the light of the tiny stump of candle, too small to be useful to humans and found on a rubbish heap, Bonaventure—his heart full of love—sat up well into the night, describing his ballet.

Monsieur Dupoint could not have known that in a mouse hole in the skirting board on the far wall of his darkened ballet school, a mouse was adding to the repertoire.

But—strangely enough—as Bonaventure, in an artistic

rapture, created a new ballet, Monsieur Dupoint was sitting in his rooms in the building directly opposite, reading the manuscript of an old one.

The manuscript was a large, yellowing softcover book filled with music and the small black marks that dancers call notation. In the candlelight, it looked holy, like a sacred text. Monsieur Dupoint gazed at it and handled it with a kind of awe. He did not know if its sacredness should inspire him with trust or fear.

Carefully he turned a page, referring to something, and then turned it back again. A delicate porcelain cup filled with rose-hip tea steamed at his right elbow, but he had forgotten it.

That afternoon, after he had finished rehearsing the *danseur* from the Company, he had crossed the street and scaled the narrow stairway to a small room at the back of the theater. Here were kept the music and the notes that recorded every ballet ever performed by the Company. It had taken him an hour to find what he was looking for; but he had found it.

Now, as he read the manuscript, he smiled gently—and wiped away a tear. He could hear the music. He could see her dancing.

But then he thought again of that final night, the night she did not rise to take her bow, and his face became troubled.

And then he thought of Clair-de-Lune.

Monsieur Dupoint closed the manuscript and laid his hands on it, palms down, as if it were some wild, unpredictable creature he wanted to pacify or appease.

"Affecting? Yes," he muttered. "Fitting? Yes. But—dangerous?" He sighed. "I fear so. And in the end, the life of a girl is more important than any dance."

❀ ❀ ❀

If Monsieur Dupoint had chanced to lean for a while on his windowsill to take the air and had glanced across to the dark casements of his ballet school, he would not have seen Bonaventure gazing out at the stars, for Bonaventure was too small and gray. But he might have seen the lithe, graceful shape of Minette moving around the outside of the building, leaping from awning to awning and picking her way across alpine slopes of slate, her green eyes reflecting any passing light.

She was accustomed to spending her nights in this exciting way.

Not for Minette the joy of The Dance, the thrill of creation. She was a consummate huntress and thus practiced instead the art of destruction.

She had checked the dancing school windows, as usual, and found them, as usual, too nearly shut for her to attempt to squeeze through. She knew a mouse lived in there, and she knew other mice were beginning to visit him. It was this, and not any interest in ballet, that made her try, over and over, to get inside the dancing school.

Mrs. Costello fed Minette better than she fed herself, for Mrs. Costello had no one to love but Minette. So Minette rarely experienced hunger.

No, Minette hunted for the thrill of it. As Leonard from the print shop might have said: each to her own.

The Last Answer—
and a New Question

All that long night, as Bonaventure was writing his ballet, as Monsieur Dupoint worried over his manuscript, and as Minette picked her way over the rooftops, Clair-de-Lune lay in bed, thinking.

At first, as she gazed through tired eyes at the dim, flickering candlelight on the ceiling—for her grandmother stayed up an hour or so after she sent Clair-de-Lune to bed—she thought of La Lune, who, it seemed, was an entirely different person from the one her grandmother had always depicted. Not a Perfect Ballerina, with no love or concern for anything but her art, but a wild girl, full of love and light, who had longed to be free and who had been forced to make a terrible choice that broke her heart.

When Clair-de-Lune thought of her mother's grief, her own heart ached so much that she thought it might break, too.

And after her grandmother went to bed and she stared

through the darkness at the stars in the small patch of sky that was visible from the window above her bed, when she could bear to think of her mother no longer, she thought of Sergei Superblatov and Lisette L'Oiseau and Eleanor Wood and the others, and felt for the first time not admiration, but a terrible pity.

As the night wore on and the stars disappeared one by one and the sky became faintly grayer, Clair-de-Lune thought, *I too can choose, I too have a choice to make.* All at once she sat up in bed and said to the dark gray sky in a soft, baby-bird voice:

I choose love.

And it seemed to her that the sky heard her, and looked kindly back.

But as she lay back down on her pillow she thought, *Perhaps, after all, I don't have to choose.*

Then the sky began to lighten, and Clair-de-Lune longed for Brother Inchmahome, for she had so much, so very much to tell him, and she knew that only he in the world would understand. *How lucky I am*, she thought, *how very lucky, despite not being able to speak, to nonetheless have someone I can talk to!*

And just at that moment, happy and at peace, she drifted off to sleep.

"Wake up, Mademoiselle Clair-de-Lune! I am too excited to sing you a lullaby! And anyway, I think that you are sad no longer! Wake up and let us repair to the monastery! For I must tell Brother Inchmahome about my latest triumphs! About the class! About my dear students! About their talent and dedication and intelligence! About the company! About my recent emergence as a choreographer! About my ballet! And about the importance of ignoring Limitations!"

Bonaventure was jumping about on the pillow next to her head, full of impatience and triumph and joy.

Clair-de-Lune dressed hurriedly and followed him out of the attic and down the stairs.

"You think it was a good class?" he asked her anxiously. "A professional class? I mean, the part of it you saw? Ah, it was a shame, was it not, that you were forced to leave us. But as I tried to convey to my dear students, they must become accustomed to those kinds of obstacles—for don't think for a moment, Mademoiselle Clair-de-Lune, that I imagine our lives as dancer mice will be easy. No," he said, as they reached the stone door and passed through it, "I fully expect that our lives will be fraught with difficulty. Ah, but I believe with all my heart that the difficulties will be well worthwhile! The excitement—the honor—of going where no mouse has gone before, and indeed of leaving a trail for the mice who come after me! When I think, mademoiselle, of the paucity of opportunities afforded to mice for artistic expression . . . Well, that is all about to change! However, being the first to do something has its drawbacks. There is no one I can consult with! I must be forever, as it were, inventing the wheel. Should mice attempt to dance as humans dance? Or should we be developing our own forms, our own steps? I am offended, for example, by the step known as *pas de chat*. Cats are no laughing matter—Brother Inchmahome!"

Brother Inchmahome, who was writing with deep concentration in a ledger on his stone desk, looked up, a little startled.

"Bonaventure, my good mouse!" he exclaimed mildly. "And Clair-de-Lune! Bonaventure, you have a triumph to share, I see!"

"Brother Inchmahome," said Bonaventure, and he scampered up onto the desk and thence, in a series of graceful leaps, to the monk's shoulder, where he was patted with great affection, "I am a teacher. A teacher of The Dance! Not only that, dear sir, but I am—as I have recently discovered—a choreographer! And soon to be a director! And I have you to thank, with all my heart, for your early advice and encouragement. Mice can dance! Mice will dance! Oh, I have such plans!"

"Congratulations, Brother Mouse," said Brother Inchmahome warmly. "Your success is well deserved. You are indeed engaged in a great work. May the good Lord bless your endeavors."

Bonaventure, who was leaning comfortably against Brother Inchmahome's neck, opened his mouth to say something, but yawned instead, and then, quite abruptly, fell asleep.

"Exhausted, no doubt," observed Brother Inchmahome. "We will let him have a little nap. It will do him good. But now," he said, turning to Clair-de-Lune, "what have you to tell me, little one? You too are tired, I can see. There are dark circles under your eyes! But you are happy, I think. . . ."

Clair-de-Lune gazed at him, her eyes shiny with tears. She suddenly felt overwhelmed with the desire to communicate, to tell him everything, and for him to know and understand.

She opened her mouth and began, in her baby-bird voice:

Brother Inchmahome . . .

But there was so much to say, about love and speaking and tinkling cymbals, about her mother and her mother's broken heart and choosing love and whether you had to choose at all; and even when she thought of any of these things on their own, or tried to, it was as if each of them had so many other things connected with them that her thoughts were like a flock of birds flying away from her, whose tail feathers she grasped at in vain with the very tips of her fingers as they escaped, leaving in their wake only a breeze and the memory of their warmth. And all the while she longed to say everything: to hold every bird in her arms and show them gently one by one while Brother Inchmahome stroked their feathered throats and fed them from his hands.

But there was also something else. Beneath these many things there was an ache, and this ache was the one thing she wanted to say more than anything else. But what was it? What was it? Even though she knew it was there somewhere, beneath the myriad other things, she could not find it, and this was the hardest thing of all.

Oh, Brother Inchmahome! she said in despair. *I have a thousand things to tell you—more than I will ever have time for in a lifetime of speaking, even if I could speak! And I have one thing to tell you, one particular thing, the most important. But I cannot find it!*

Brother Inchmahome smiled slowly, and even a little sadly.

"Ah, Clair-de-Lune!" he said. "No, you will never say all the things you have to say, for even in a lifetime of speaking, there is not enough time. That, I fear, is something you must simply learn to live with, and perhaps it will always be a great sadness to someone who wants to speak as much as you do. But then it is no reason not to speak at all. And perhaps it would be more useful for you to turn your attention to that which is essential, for very few things are, you know. Which brings me to the second part of what you just said.

"Clair-de-Lune, you have given me the last answer! And so—now that you have told me all the reasons that you cannot speak—I must change my question." He leaned forward on the stone desk, his arms folded beneath him, his face very earnest. "What is it that you want to say?"

Clair-de-Lune gazed at him across the desk. She saw the calmness and alertness in Brother Inchmahome's face, the profound interest in his eyes. And somehow his kindness to her burned and ached inside her, and she knew that this burning and aching was the thing she so wanted to say. But although she felt that this thing was so familiar she had always known it, it also seemed to her to be so strange that she would not find it, even if she were to travel to the moon.

What was it? What was it?

She looked at him helplessly and shook her head.

I don't know, she said at last. *I don't know!*

"Ah," said Brother Inchmahome, "but you do, Clair-de-Lune! Do not be afraid." And suddenly she felt that he was listening to something, something he couldn't quite hear. "For now, at last," he said softly, "we have come to the heart of the matter. Or it has come to us!

"You see, my dear—if I may be frank—although you think your difficulty is that you cannot speak, I am not so sure. I never have been. I think your difficulty is that you do not know how to listen.

"And in order to speak truly, one must first learn to listen."

Clair-de-Lune stared at him, dismayed.

Listen? she said. *But listen to what?*

"First," said Brother Inchmahome simply, "one's own heart. And after that, whatever or whoever speaks to you."

Clair-de-Lune's heart was pounding. She found something about what Brother Inchmahome was saying deeply frightening. And she also felt a kind of despair. What if she could not do it?

"But I can see that you are alarmed—you must not be alarmed! You see, Clair-de-Lune, there is one thing you listen to all the time. It is fear. Do not listen to fear. . . ."

But again Clair-de-Lune saw that he was listening to something he could not quite hear, and in the clear dawn sky of his eyes there was pain.

"If only we could protect those we love," he murmured, so softly that she could barely hear him. Suddenly she felt as if she were setting out on a long journey. She was about to ask another question when all at once, as she looked into Brother Inchmahome's eyes, she saw, for just a moment, an extraordinary thing: a young man, peeking out from behind something, watching her shyly, about to speak. No sooner had she seen him than he was gone.

Brother Inchmahome— she began.

"Ah, but enough of this idle chatter!" said Bonaventure suddenly as he awoke. "I shall be late! Mademoiselle shall be late! Thank you again, Brother Inchmahome, with all my heart! *Adieu!*"

"You are very welcome, Brother Mouse," said Brother Inchmahome softly, for the mouse had already gone. "*Bon voyage*, Clair-de-Lune!"

And so Clair-de-Lune followed Bonaventure out through the long corridor, past the porter, through the garden with the sea on her right and the blue sky above her, and through the black oblong that was the door back into her other life. Then, as usual, she went upstairs to the attic to get changed for her class, and Bonaventure went downstairs to get ready for his.

As Clair-de-Lune dressed, her face was solemn. She was only one step from her goal.

But although she knew the step to be a large one, she never could have dreamed what adventures were still to come.

Listening

All that day, Clair-de-Lune listened.

She listened to her grandmother at breakfast—to her severity and austerity and tenacity—and thought for the first time, with surprise, *My grandmama is sad*.

She listened to the girls at the dancing school—to Milly Twinkenham, Fenella Flynn, and Prudence Eeling especially— and not just to what they said. She listened to what she knew about them, although she had rarely allowed herself to think it. *They are afraid of me,* she thought. *More afraid, even, than I am of them!*

Although, to be honest, this didn't make her fear them any less.

Still, somehow, their dislike of her didn't seem to matter so much anymore. For nothing mattered but love. Her mother had thought so, too!

So on this extraordinary morning, as she passed Milly on her way into class, she caught her eye and smiled her crooked little smile at her. And Milly was so taken aback that for once she was speechless.

There were six boys in Monsieur Dupoint's class. Clair-de-Lune had never taken any notice of them before, but now that she listened to them, she thought with surprise that they seemed . . . kind.

"Don't worry—I'll lend you mine," said one to another, and just then he suddenly looked up and saw her watching him. Being a pleasant boy by nature, and not knowing what else to do, he smiled uncertainly; promptly, Clair-de-Lune smiled crookedly back. She was beginning to get the hang of it.

She listened to Monsieur Dupoint, and thought, *He is worried.*

She listened to Mr. Sparrow at the piano and heard for the first time, beneath the music, the faint sound of his fingers as they hit the keys, and the sound of the piano stool creaking as he changed position.

She listened for Bonaventure—and fancied she could just hear (though this may have been her imagination) the tiny sound of his voice squeaking with excitement as he announced a glorious new project to his students, who had gathered, one by one, secretly, for a meeting in his mouse hole.

And she tried listening to her own heart.

But that was more difficult.

When Clair-de-Lune set out for the market that afternoon, she was surprised to pass Monsieur Dupoint on the stairs.

"Ah! Good afternoon, child!" he said.

Clair-de-Lune bobbed a curtsy in reply and noticed not

only that he was wearing his top hat, gloves, and good black frock coat, but that he seemed startled to see her.

He is visiting someone, she thought as she continued down the stairs. *Could it be my grandmama?*

But then, of course, the building was full of people. He could have been visiting any of them.

Monsieur Dupoint *had* been startled, for he had been thinking of Clair-de-Lune at precisely the moment she rounded the corner.

"Poor child," he muttered, taking the stairs two at a time. But he wasn't thinking of her muteness.

When he reached the sixth floor, he paused for a moment to catch his breath and collect himself. He had a difficult task before him. Then he raised his hand and knocked on Clair-de-Lune's grandmother's door.

"Come in," said the old lady's voice, sounding cold and a little surprised.

Monsieur Dupoint popped his head round the door.

"Madame," he said respectfully. "Er—may I . . . ?"

"Monsieur Dupoint!" exclaimed Clair-de-Lune's grandmother. "Come in, of course. Do sit down. Tea?"

"No. Thank you, madame." And Clair-de-Lune's grandmother sighed inwardly with relief, for had he said yes, she would have had no cake to offer him with it. A cake was too expensive to keep just for visitors. And visitors were so rare! Clair-de-Lune's grandmother had begun discouraging them shortly after her daughter's death.

"I hope, madame, that you will forgive this intrusion. I find you well, I hope?"

"Very well, monsieur, thank you."

"I am glad to hear it. . . . Er, forgive, as I say, this intrusion, but I need to consult with you on a matter of some importance. It is also, madame—I should warn you—a matter that, though essentially good news, may cause you distress by reviving . . . er, sad memories."

Clair-de-Lune's grandmother sat still and spare and straight-backed in her chair. The afternoon sun poured in through the latticed window behind her. In her black dress and lace shawl, she looked like an elegant shadow. She gazed at him through her large, sad, dark eyes.

"Pray continue, monsieur. I am strong."

Monsieur Dupoint shifted in his seat and cleared his throat.

"Madame," he began gently, "as you are no doubt aware, the Company's hundredth anniversary falls in May, and it is to be celebrated with a special performance, which will include tributes to our greatest achievements, past and present. No such celebration would be complete, of course, without some reference to La Lune—the brightest of our stars—"

"Indeed," muttered Clair-de-Lune's grandmother.

"—and it has been suggested to me that her dance—the dance with which we all associate her most keenly—"

"Her last dance," said Clair-de-Lune's grandmother coldly.

"Yes," said Monsieur Dupoint bravely, "her last dance—that it should be revived. Now of course the Company has several first-rate principals, all of whom, in their own ways, would dance a beautiful tribute to our dear girl. But Monsieur le Directeur feels—indeed, I believe the Company as a whole thinks—in short, it has been suggested to me that no one would be so appropriate to revive La Lune's dance as La Lune's daughter."

Monsieur Dupoint looked alertly at the old lady. He was sitting forward, on the edge of his chair, his hands spread on his knees.

Madame Nuit sat as still and straight as a statue. Her face was almost inscrutable. But—just perceptibly—it had paled. The wound of her daughter's death was for her, even after twelve years, so fresh that the very mention of her name made the room spin. For a moment, she thought she would faint.

Discipline, she thought. *Discipline*.

As she fought for self-control, her heart ached and ached, and then, all at once, flared in anger. Revive her daughter's dance? How dare they? So, they thought they had a replacement, did they? Or worse, a successor! Furious, she thought of the Company's current crop of dancers—mere starlets, glorified *cancan* dancers. How was it that they were so blind? La Lune was irreplaceable! She had no successor.

Except—

And then the room began to spin more slowly, like a merry-go-round at the end of the ride, and the old lady understood what Monsieur Dupoint had been saying, and murmured distantly.

"Clair-de-Lune?"

It is as I hoped, thought Monsieur Dupoint, who had been trying to read her face. *She does not approve.* He sighed with relief.

"I am," he said, "I must confess, uneasy about this idea, madame. Decidedly uneasy. First of all, Clair-de-Lune is a child: she is by no means fully formed as a dancer. Of course, it would be a most moving tribute, precisely because she is a child and has such promise! But performing too early can stunt an artist's growth. She should not grow up trying to please an audience. Let that come when she is fully in command of her powers—and strong enough to be herself, no matter what they think.

"But even more importantly, madame—what of the personal dimension to all this? Surely it would be too painful, both for yourself and for Clair-de-Lune. I must admit to you, madame, that I am a little concerned about the child. She seems . . . well, the nervous strain involved in taking on such a task, in learning and performing the very dance that . . . Well, such an undertaking would seem to me likely to be injurious to the child's best interests, as I'm sure you will agree.

"And there is something else, if I may beg your patience, madame."

"Yes?" the old lady whispered. She seemed spellbound.

"If it goes ahead, I will of course take responsibility for the performance. And so I will be coaching Clair-de-Lune from the manuscript Monsieur de la Croix left among his papers. How can I put this? The theater, you know, is a place haunted by superstition, and although I do not hold with such nonsense, I must tell you that a certain peculiar anxiety with regard to reviving the very dance that—"

Monsieur Dupoint broke off and raised his arms expressively.

"I think they call it numinous dread," he said. "Suffice it to say I am uneasy. And yet, what am I against the director, the Company? However"—and here he leaned forward—"if I had your support . . . if you were to express your disapproval . . . I am sure they would drop the idea. You have only to say the word, madame, and I will fight for you."

He paused, looking expectantly at her.

Clair-de-Lune's grandmother gazed back at him. She felt as if she were standing on a precipice. To say what she wanted to say would be to step over the edge. And yet she said it.

"She will do it," she breathed.

For a moment the room was completely silent.

"Madame," faltered Monsieur Dupoint, "I'm not sure I—"

"You heard me correctly, monsieur. I said she will do it."

"But madame—I thought—you are quite certain? You do not want a little time to—consider?"

"Your sensitivity does you credit, monsieur. I have never doubted that you were a good friend to my daughter, and indeed to Clair-de-Lune. But I am quite certain."

"But—you are not concerned that—"

"Monsieur Dupoint," said Clair-de-Lune's grandmother softly, wearily, in a voice that was almost kind, "it was not The Dance that killed my daughter. She died—I know—of a broken heart. She was killed by her love for a disreputable young man. Clair-de-Lune is in no danger. She loves no one. I have made sure of it."

She held Monsieur Dupoint's eyes until he dropped them, confused and abashed.

He was shocked by what she had said, and yet he felt powerless, defeated. Her conviction was such that his withered before it.

His manners had deserted him; he searched in vain first for something to say that might change her mind, and then in sheer desperation—for he was a polite and very respectful man—for some kind of small talk to make the situation less awkward.

But he need not have worried. Madame Nuit was so lost in her thoughts that she barely noticed him, and seemed startled when, finally, he took his leave.

He went helplessly down the stairs, twirling his hat nervously in his hands, feeling more and more uneasy.

There was nothing he could do. If it must go ahead, he had to cooperate, had to agree to coach the child. For if he were to refuse—if they gave the job to someone else—

Then there would be no one to protect her.

But the thing that worried him most was that of all the reasons he had given, all the proof that it was a bad idea, the one that held most weight for him was the last.

"And I have never been superstitious," he muttered.

He passed Clair-de-Lune on the stairs again as he descended.

"Oh—good evening, child," he said unhappily.

As he disappeared round the corner of the next landing,

Clair-de-Lune stood quite still, watching after him, and biting her lip.

When Clair-de-Lune opened the door to the attic a moment later, she was so startled by her grandmother's appearance that her heart came into her mouth. The room was filled with afternoon sunlight; her grandmother was sitting farther toward the center than usual, and opposite another, empty chair. In her black dress, against the glow of the light, she did indeed look like a shadow, a little piece of night in the midst of day.

Clair-de-Lune's grandmother looked up vaguely.

"Come in, child, and put your parcels on the table. I have news."

Her heart thudding softly, Clair-de-Lune obeyed. For a moment she hesitated, lingering at the table, her head down. Then, dragging her hands from the parcels, she moved—one step, two steps—toward her grandmother and stood before her, her eyes on the floor, her hands clasped on her skirt.

"You have been accorded a great honor," began her grandmother, looking not at her but through her at someone else (and although that person was not present, Clair-de-Lune knew who she was). "Your great mother's *pas seul*—the one for which she sacrificed her young life—is to be revived for the Company's centenary. You are to dance it. You are not yet the dancer your mother was—far from it. But you must try with all your heart to be worthy of her, and of the Company, and of the honor. Now you will practice the pianoforte, we will eat supper, and you will go early to bed. Monsieur Dupoint will want to start rehearsing you tomorrow."

But Clair-de-Lune could not eat her supper, and as she lay in bed that night, she was in such pain that she wondered if she could ever be happy again.

It was not the dancing, nor the thought of performing for the first time for an audience. They were nothing, nothing.

No. The thing that was so painful to her—so painful that she could barely hold it in her head—was that by dancing her mother's dance, she would be forced, in her heart, to relive her mother's death.

She did not know how she was going to go through with it.

It seemed to her that every step would be agony, would tear her apart.

For here it was at last—the muffled voice that had frightened her all her life. It seemed strange to her now that she had ever been in any doubt about the horrible thing it had been trying to say. She knew what it was now. It was trying to talk to her about her mother's death.

And it seemed to Clair-de-Lune that this great shadow had moved between her and the sun forever.

Not Listening

At two o'clock the following afternoon, Clair-de-Lune was warming up at the *barre*. From now until Monsieur Dupoint was satisfied with her performance, she was to do her morning class, then go upstairs for lunch, and return in the afternoon for a two-hour rehearsal. The errands would have to be run later, and for some weeks she would be missing out on her lessons.

What will keep me sensible now? thought Clair-de-Lune as she moved automatically from first into second position and continued her *pliés*.

She had seen, the moment she crept into the room, that Monsieur Dupoint was angry. She could not have known this, but Monsieur Dupoint was the kind of person who tended to become angry when in fact he was feeling sympathetic or protective toward someone. He grunted at her as she arrived, and muttered, "Weeks! A matter of weeks! And they expect me to get a mere child up to professional standard! The very idea is preposterous!" And he glared, for no reason at all, at poor

Mr. Sparrow, who was sitting at the piano looking even sadder than usual.

"Affecting! Fitting! Hmpf!" concluded Monsieur Dupoint, and buried himself again in the large, yellowing manuscript that he held carefully in his hands.

Clair-de-Lune did not want to look at the manuscript, and yet as she continued her warm-up she found her eyes drawn toward it despite herself. She knew that written in it was the notation that recorded the choreography of her mother's last dance.

The dance had been created by an elderly gentleman, a former *danseur*, by the name of Gilbert de la Croix, who had since died.

There was a window dedicated to him at St. Mary's down the road.

If Clair-de-Lune had been able to speak—and if (more importantly) she had ever found her grandmother persuadable on any decision once made—she would have begged on her knees to be spared this ordeal. But she could not speak, and her grandmother was not persuadable, and Clair-de-Lune felt strangely hopeless, trapped. She felt that the most terrible of all her fears had at last caught up with her. It was as if this had been waiting for her all along, and all her progress—all her mornings with Brother Inchmahome—counted for nothing against it.

Worst of all, although she had visited Brother Inchmahome this morning, as usual, with Bonaventure, she had not been able to make him understand her—he who, till now, had understood everything.

"What can be wrong, little one?" he had asked with concern.

But Clair-de-Lune had shaken her head hopelessly. For something had come to claim her, something from so long ago, so far back, that Brother Inchmahome's listening could not reach it.

Now she was utterly alone.

"Clair-de-Lune? Into the center now, child. Mr. Sparrow will play the music right through for you. Then we will study it, and the steps, section by section. Listen carefully. Mr. Sparrow?"

Slowly, sadly, Clair-de-Lune let go of the *barre* and crept into the center. Young Mr. Sparrow, his face solemn, intent, began to play, and soon became lost in the music. Monsieur Dupoint was staring at the ceiling, counting under his breath.

But Clair-de-Lune stood in the center of the floor—as the music pit-patted over her like little fingers, like the softest of rain—shaking from head to toe.

It was the music. She had known it from the first note. It was the piece he had played the day she had cried, the day she had met Bonaventure, the day her learning to speak had begun.

She had not known!

She had thought it the most beautiful music she had ever heard, but she had not known it was her mother's dance.

And now, all at once, it was here, it was present—not just a fear, but a danger as real as a fierce animal in the room. It was as if there were in the music an emotion so intense that, were she to give way to it, she would die. It was as if there were a voice in the music that was begging and begging to be heard, but if heard, would destroy her.

Clair-de-Lune looked wildly around the room. She had two impulses: to cover her ears with her hands and to run away—out of the room, down the stairs, out of the building, and away, never to return. But she resisted both.

For there was only one real way to protect herself.

When Monsieur Dupoint looked down at her he was startled: for he saw that although standing still neatly in first position, the child was rigid with effort.

He assumed, tenderheartedly, that it was her wish to excel at her mother's dance, and his bad mood began to soften.

But in fact Clair-de-Lune was rigid with the effort of not listening.

"Now, child," Monsieur Dupoint said as Mr. Sparrow finished playing and glanced up at him, "Mr. Sparrow will play one section at a time, and I will show you the steps. First I will dance, then you will dance." He stood beside her, drew himself up, nodded at Mr. Sparrow, and demonstrated the first little sequence of steps.

But, although he demonstrated the *enchaînement* beautifully, he was not dancing as himself. He was imitating his memory of La Lune.

"*Bourrée, bourrée, bourrée*—arms up slowly, and—down

144

and fold against the breast," he said, in rhythm with the music. He finished, and Mr. Sparrow stopped playing abruptly, leaving the music in the air. "Now you try. The piece is deceptively simple throughout but demands great control and, most of all, feeling. Mr. Sparrow?"

The music began again. This time it was Clair-de-Lune who danced.

"*Bourrée, bourrée, bourrée*—that's right, slowly—down and fold against—good. Remember, the arms are always in motion—they perfect one attitude only to develop continually into the next. Now the next part: watch me. Mr. Sparrow?"

And so it went on. First Monsieur Dupoint would dance, imitating his memory of La Lune. Then Clair-de-Lune would dance, imitating Monsieur Dupoint. Every so often Monsieur Dupoint would stop, walk briskly over to the piano, and consult the manuscript.

"Ah, yes," he would mutter; then he would come back and alter something he had taught her. Obediently, Clair-de-Lune would change the step, too.

But as she danced, Clair-de-Lune was clenching her teeth so hard that her whole skull ached.

As the rehearsal progressed, Monsieur Dupoint grew more and more cheerful.

For the child was dancing well—better than he had ever seen her dance before—and Monsieur Dupoint's misgivings, grave though they were, were not proof against his pride in his pupil.

It was easy for Clair-de-Lune to learn her mother's dance— so easy it was frightening. It was as if she already knew it.

But that was not the reason she was dancing so well.

The reason was that she had never in her life concentrated so hard; she had never in her life thought so exclusively about rhythm and movement and nothing else. She had become a dancing doll. For she knew that as soon as she stopped concentrating and became a living, breathing girl again, the meaning of what she was doing would flood her, and she would be lost.

The hardest part of all was the end.

"Down, down, down—slide forward, that's right—and the head slowly . . . falls, and is still. The swan is dying, you see, but even to the end, she fights. She wants to live. It is important to remember that, Clair-de-Lune. The swan is dying, but she wants to live."

And by this time Monsieur Dupoint was so involved in the rehearsal and in teaching her that he was no longer thinking of her mother, only of the dance itself—almost as if it had no history and was being created for the first time now, here, in front of him.

But Clair-de-Lune could not forget, and the effort not to listen—or at least to listen only with her head and not her heart—was, at this point, almost beyond her strength.

When at last the rehearsal finished and the music stopped, Clair-de-Lune was as pale as death.

"Excellent!" said Monsieur Dupoint, so glowing with his pupil's progress that he did not notice. "You have your dear mother's talent, my child! Now go home and be sure to eat a good dinner. Then rest. You have earned the sleep of the angels!"

But as Clair-de-Lune meekly performed her *révérence*, first to Monsieur Dupoint and then to Mr. Sparrow at the piano, Monsieur Dupoint was surprised by the sudden shudder of fear that passed over him. All at once, he was in a bad mood again. He glared at Mr. Sparrow. Hurriedly, Mr. Sparrow packed up his music, shut the piano, and followed Clair-de-Lune out the door.

Monsieur Dupoint sat alone in his empty classroom, staring moodily out the window.

And Bonaventure, who had seen all from the doorway of his mouse hole, sat trying to understand what he had seen.

Meanwhile, out on the stairs, just around the corner between the first and second flight above the dancing school, Clair-de-Lune had collapsed, shuddering and sobbing in weak little gasps.

There would be weeks and weeks of this. How would she bear it?

But bear it she did, for (as I have said before) Clair-de-Lune had a will of iron. She could not disobey her grandmother; she could not disappoint Monsieur Dupoint and the Company; she could not dishonor her mother's memory.

As the weeks passed, however, it seemed to her that her heart was breaking. For in order to keep faith with all these, in order merely to survive, she had been forced to betray something else. And the thing she was betraying was far more important.

And so day folded into night and bloomed as day again, and Clair-de-Lune slept, visited Brother Inchmahome, went to class, rehearsed her mother's dance, ran her errands, and slept again. She ate little and grew even thinner, and she listened to nothing, for she could not afford to.

Monsieur Dupoint was astonished at her progress. But as the date of the performance grew nearer and nearer, he began to realize that something was missing. Not only that: he knew what it was.

She has steeled herself, he thought in wonder as he watched her one afternoon. *She has steeled herself against the pain. Technically she is as good as a child her age could be. But there is no feeling in what she is doing. And her mother,* he reflected, *was all feeling.*

But although the dance was so important to him and he knew Clair-de-Lune was capable of more, the fact that she was approaching it in this way pleased him, and he began to feel a little less anxious. For if Clair-de-Lune could get through the performance, just going through the motions—which, after all, was all that could be expected of a child—he knew she would be safe.

He imagined that it was easy to dance in this way, without feeling. But he did not know how much strength it took. And the cruelest thing of all, for Clair-de-Lune, was that she could no longer speak to Brother Inchmahome, not even as a baby bird—or at least she could say nothing of what was in her heart.

For it was true. When one cannot listen, one cannot speak.

Meanwhile, as Clair-de-Lune rehearsed for her professional debut, Bonaventure was working toward his. He had seized upon the Company's centenary as the perfect occasion for the first performance of his new ballet and had been working on it, with his dancers, day and night. As he rehearsed them, he would revise it, for he often found that things looked different in performance than they had in his head, and also, if he discovered a strength in someone, he liked to use it and would immediately write it in.

For example, when he discovered just how high young Rudolph could jump, the ballet quickly developed a subplot. The Mouse Prince had a loyal friend who would accompany him on his quest! And when he saw the exceptional expressiveness of Margot's whiskers, he choreographed a special solo for her: she was the Mouse Lady's vivacious lady-in-waiting.

He hesitated to attempt a role himself. In fact, he had planned only to direct, and thought he would have his paws full just doing that. But his company had insisted. No one, they said, could dance the Mouse Prince as well as he. And so he had bowed to their better judgment and thrown himself into the role. The Mouse Lady was to be danced by little Juliet from the print shop. She was the most graceful of them all and had the most astonishingly lyrical tail Bonaventure had ever seen. Juliet's tail, Bonaventure believed, could have told an entire story all by itself.

The score for *The Prince's Quest* had been written by the brilliant, deaf mouse who lived in the organ at St. Mary's. She had composed it entirely in her head and was playing for rehearsals on a toy piano Bonaventure had found in a toy shop. Money is not of much value to mice, but a mouse can always tell you where it can be found: there are always coins that have rolled into gutters, or down behind furniture, or under floor-boards. Bonaventure was able to collect enough of these stray coins from his students—and from his own sources—to place them as payment on the shelf where the little piano had lived before he and some burly mouse friends removed it in the dead of one moonlit night and hoisted it, with some difficulty, up the stairs and into its new home. He had found musicians—though he had had to travel as far as two streets away to find them—and still other mice were designing costumes and back-drops.

But he had yet to find a suitable venue.

One evening, as he sat working on his revisions, he suddenly looked up, his eyes bright with inspiration.

"Of course!" he said aloud. "Why did I not think of it before?"

The evening star rose in the sky outside. But Bonaventure was not at the window to see it.

That same evening, Clair-de-Lune's grandmother bade her climb onto the table and lift down a large, tall, cylindrical box that sat on the very top of the cupboard, near the press clippings. It was awkward to carry, but it was not heavy. Clair-de-Lune set it on the table and hopped down from the chair.

Her grandmother's face was particularly stony. Clair-de-Lune had not known what was in the box, but now, looking at her grandmother, she knew; she knew.

"Open the box, child, and take out what you find there," said her grandmother.

Clair-de-Lune opened it and found, as she had expected, a

long white *tutu*, folded inside out. But even though she had known what she was going to find, when the lid came off and she saw it for the first time, she was startled, for in the candlelight it looked like nothing so much as a dead swan.

"Take it out and put it on," said her grandmother.

Clair-de-Lune took it out carefully, and even more carefully pulled it right way out. It was beautiful, of course—but it made her uneasy, for there was something else it reminded her of, something she could not quite place. Clair-de-Lune climbed out of her dress and stepped into it, pulling it up over her stockings and slipping her arms through the delicate sleeves.

It was the feel of it—the layers upon layers of tulle and swans' feathers—that made her realize.

The *tutu* reminded her of the stuff that had always seemed to muffle that voice—the terrifying voice that wanted to tell her about her mother's death.

How strange that the voice should seem buried beneath a pretty thing like a *tutu*!

"Turn around, child," said her grandmother, and the old lady fastened it up the back, hook into eye, hook into eye.

"Now let me see you."

Clair-de-Lune turned to face her. The *tutu* was too big for her, of course, but not as much as you might imagine, for Clair-de-Lune's mother had been barely eighteen when she died, and she had been small and thin. In the candlelight, Clair-de-Lune did not look like a child wearing an adult's dress. Instead, the *tutu* simply made Clair-de-Lune look older.

Clair-de-Lune's grandmother gazed at her for a moment

without comment. Then she opened her sewing basket and began to pin the *tutu* in, to fit Clair-de-Lune's form.

For this, too—the dress La Lune had died in—was to be altered to fit her daughter.

Clair-de-Lune sat with Brother Inchmahome in the sea garden. The night of the performance was less than a week away now, and Bonaventure was off on a mysterious errand. His premiere, too, was approaching. Time was running out! So Clair-de-Lune and Brother Inchmahome were alone.

"Clair-de-Lune," said Brother Inchmahome with the air of one who had finally decided to say something, "you are paler than ever, and thinner than ever, and you do not tell me anything anymore. I have been wondering whether what I said some weeks ago about listening did you more harm than good. I am wondering if I have taken your confidence away. For listening, you know, should not be a burden. Indeed, Clair-de-Lune, listening is a liberation! Perhaps I did not explain myself well enough."

But Clair-de-Lune shook her head listlessly.

It is not that, she said softly, in the voice of a baby bird who hungers and yet fears that its mother will not return to her nest. *It is simply, dear Brother Inchmahome, that as soon as you told me about listening, I came upon something impossible to listen to. And now it seems to me that I must fail—that I will never listen, and thus I will never truly speak. For now that I know what listening is, I know that if I listen, I will die.*

"But, Clair-de-Lune," said Brother Inchmahome earnestly, "listening is not death. Listening is life!"

Listening is terror, said Clair-de-Lune, and it was the first time she had ever contradicted him.

"Listening is love," said Brother Inchmahome, and suddenly there were tears in his voice. "And love can be frightening. But love is always good, Clair-de-Lune. And love is more important than anything. We must be open to it. We must not shut it out—no matter what the consequences. You are fighting something, my dear. Do not fight. Listen."

And as Clair-de-Lune stared at him, the tears rolling down her cheeks, she knew, at last, what she had to do.

The Locket

Late, late that night, Clair-de-Lune slept in the attic. Through the latticed window, the moon shone onto her still face, its long white fingers resting coolly on her forehead, stroking her cheek, smoothing her hair. Clair-de-Lune's eyes fluttered open. For just a moment she lay still. Then, silently, she rose from her bed. She pulled the cover off and wrapped it around herself. Then, on her bare feet, she crept over to the table.

Here, folded inside out and sitting up stiffly, was her mother's swan *tutu*, now altered to fit Clair-de-Lune. A new pair of pink satin *pointe* shoes lay beside it. Clair-de-Lune gathered the dress up and laid the shoes on top. She hesitated for a moment, glancing across at her grandmother. Then she set out.

Down the stairs she went, all twelve flights of them, and finally out onto the cobbled street. The night air was cold, and of course there was no market, only the shadows of the empty stalls. Clair-de-Lune did not pause. She crossed the narrow street and, coming to the back of the theater, let herself in through the stage door. She had been given a key by Monsieur

Dupoint that very afternoon; all the principals had one. But Clair-de-Lune had a special use for it, a special need of it.

When she had shut the door behind her, she found herself in total darkness. But Clair-de-Lune knew her way. And she was not afraid. Cradling the *tutu* and the shoes carefully in one arm, the bedcover draped like a shawl over her shoulders, she felt her way across the small lobby and up the stairs. If she had been going to the dressing rooms, she would have turned right here and continued down the hall. But instead she climbed a second short flight of stairs. Now the dark began to lessen, and Clair-de-Lune feared for a moment that despite the lateness of the hour, she was not alone. But when she reached the top of the stairs and crept into the wings—for now she was backstage—she saw instead a strange thing.

High in the wall, in the wings on the opposite side of the stage, there was a window. And through this window—also latticed—the moon shone so brightly that the stage was lit up, as if by the gentlest of spotlights.

Clair-de-Lune gazed up at it.

Then, slowly, she stepped onto the stage.

The audience was a vast black cavern, as vast and as black as the night sky; the stage was a room of light, a room of moonlight, suspended in it. For a moment Clair-de-Lune stood motionless in wonder, cradling her mother's *tutu* to her breast.

Then, busily, with new purpose, she stepped back into the wings, put the *tutu* on the floor, laid the shoes beside it, and peeled off her nightgown. Carefully, she unfolded her mother's dress and pulled it on. She thought she would not be able to do it up by herself, but everything seemed easy tonight.

155

When she had put on her shoes, crisscrossing the ribbons low on her ankles, over the stockings she had been wearing under her nightgown, she used the *barre* backstage to warm up.

Then, a dancer now, she stepped onto the stage. She folded her arms on her breast and rose *en pointe*. Then the music began in her head.

And now, alone, in her mother's dress, on the stage where her mother had died, she danced her mother's dance—not as she had danced it when she was afraid, but as she knew it should be danced.

She was a swan. . . .

And she was dying. . . .

But though she was dying, she wanted to live. And so she fought it—the weakness, the weight, the torpor that made it more and more difficult to lift her wings. Even when every movement was agony, still she would not give in, although the music was urging her to, was singing a lullaby, was saying, *Rest, rest, fear no more, rest*—

But swans, it is said, sing—and only once in their lives, while they are dying.

So Clair-de-Lune listened, listened with all her heart. For this was her mother's dance, and she was speaking to Clair-de-Lune through it. As she listened, with more courage than she had ever had to draw on before this night, it seemed to her that the layers and layers that had muffled that voice melted away. And when they had melted, the voice was not frightening at all.

As the dance drew to a close; as the swan sank down, defeated at last, and the music sang a farewell to her; as Clair-de-

Lune slid forward onto the boards, extended her leg and brought her fluttering arms out in front of her, and finally laid her head down among the tulle of her skirt, she knew what her mother was saying.

At last the music in her head was silent. For a moment Clair-de-Lune lay crumpled on the stage, flooded in moonlight.

Then she lifted her head and stared straight up at the moon in wonder.

But how could that be? she whispered, a baby bird's whisper, into the utter silence. *You did not even know him!*

Like one in a dream, she picked herself up, crept backstage, took off the *tutu*, and turned it inside out. Then she put her nightgown back on, wrapped the bedcover around herself, bundled up her belongings, and departed.

She had listened with all her heart, and she had heard something, too—so clearly that it could not be mistaken.

But she did not understand. She did not understand.

She was so distracted by her thoughts that she did not even glance back at the stage. If she had, she might have noticed something lying on it.

For something, a little glinting silver thing, had fallen from Clair-de-Lune's mother's *tutu* as she had been dancing. Clair-de-Lune's mother had sewn it herself into the lining. But it had been twelve years, and the silk had become weak, and anyway, La Lune had never been much good at sewing.

Clair-de-Lune did not see the little glinting silver thing. But someone else did. For Clair-de-Lune had not, after all, been alone in the theater. Bonaventure had been with her and, from the wings on the opposite side of the stage, had seen all.

For this was the stage on which Bonaventure intended his ballet to have its premiere: the stage of all stages, the stage of the theater that housed the Company itself! Of course, certain adaptations would need to be made. It was so big—impossibly big for a company of mice. But then, Bonaventure was expecting a large audience, for the number of mice living in the district around the theater was considerable. Thus he planned to build a mouse-sized stage on the stage itself, out of several shoe boxes—easy both to assemble and to take away overnight. The audience would gather around them. The stage would be lit by tiny candles, around which rose petals would be scattered artistically. And the performance would take place on the night of the centenary celebration, beginning at the moment the last human left the theater.

Bonaventure was hoping Clair-de-Lune could find a way to attend.

But when he had seen her here tonight, he had been mystified.

What could have brought her here, alone, in the middle of the night? He himself was here on business, after all; he kept coming back to look at the stage as work on his mouse ballet progressed. He needed to remember its vastness, draw in its atmosphere.

But Clair-de-Lune?

As he watched her performance, however, he thought he understood. For she was dancing so differently! Bonaventure had not understood the dance, as danced in Monsieur

Dupoint's classroom, at all. He had thought it must have been some peculiar piece about a mechanical bird, and he could not understand the reason for its reputation.

But when he saw Clair-de-Lune dance it on her own . . .

How sublime it was! How moving! Bonaventure was touched to the quick, and brushed tears away from his fur.

Of course! Her interpretation was too delicate, too personal to be exposed to a common rehearsal! But secretly, in her heart, and here on her own, she had worked on it, and on the night of the performance, it would blossom!

When she finished, it was all Bonaventure could do to stop himself applauding. Then he realized that she might be upset by his presence, so he kept quiet.

But when she rose and walked offstage, he saw the thing that had fallen from her costume.

He waited until she had disappeared down the stairs. He scurried over to investigate. And then he sat looking at it, his black eyes puzzled.

It was a small, heart-shaped locket; and when it had fallen, the locket had come open. So now Bonaventure was staring at a miniature: a picture of a person that to a human being would have been small, but which to a mouse was as large as a gallery-sized portrait.

There was something . . . familiar about the face.

In fact . . .

Bonaventure sat forward, peering intently into the tiny silver compartment.

For just a moment, the depth of his surprise and mystification made him hesitate.

Then, decisively, he reached out his paws and shut the locket carefully, with a click, to keep what was inside it safe. He did not understand, though he knew it was important and must be returned to Clair-de-Lune. But just as he went to pick it up—

A large, soft paw descended gracefully and pinned it to the stage.

The moon had sunk out of sight now, and the night was black. But Bonaventure's night vision was good, and so when he looked up, he recognized Mrs. Costello's Minette.

Mrs. Costello's Minette crouched neatly and patiently on the stage, her tail batting gently back and forth. For a moment, unguardedly, Bonaventure looked into her eyes, and even for that briefest of moments he began to feel himself drawn into them, as a drowning creature is drawn under the waves. But then he pulled himself out again and stared at the locket.

There are times in life when choices seem very clear. A mouse is always close to death, for a mouse is always in danger. But Bonaventure wanted to live! There was his company, and his ballet, and The Dance! *Perhaps,* he thought in that split second, *I should not worry about the locket. It will encumber me— and perhaps, without it, I will get away.*

But what if, regardless, I do not get away, and what if the locket is lost forever? She might never see it, he thought. *She might never know. . . .*

Love is more important than The Dance, thought Bonaventure, and he darted to one side, the side of the paw that had trapped the locket. The cat lifted her paw to prevent his escape; in the twinkling of an eye, Bonaventure changed direction, seized the locket, and was off, hurtling across the stage, down the stairs, and out under the door.

But Minette knew enough about Bonaventure's day-to-day movements to have a shrewd idea where he was headed. And besides, she knew a shortcut.

Unhurried, she set off in the opposite direction, the way she had come in. A stepladder rested against the far wall; she scaled it and escaped through the high window, the window through which the moon had been shining. But now the sky was already streaked with dawn.

Minette went swiftly as a shadow over the roof of the theater. Then—for, remember, the street was narrow and the roofs crammed across the sky—in one magnificent leap she jumped from the roof of the theater to the roof of Clair-de-Lune's building. Minette thought nothing of it. She did it every night. She came in through the window of the landing outside Clair-de-Lune's door, jumped down onto the staircase, and sat washing herself as she waited.

Mice don't think like cats. Cats are creatures of strategy; mice just act. Bonaventure had one thought in his head: to get the locket to Clair-de-Lune. He had hurtled down the stairs, under the door, across the street, into the building, and up the stairs along the banisters, awkward and not as fast as usual owing to his burden, which he carried between his teeth. He had not, of course, forgotten the cat, but, thinking like a mouse, he had thought she would chase him. He little imagined he was running right into her paws.

When, exhausted, he rounded the corner and came to the last flight of stairs, the one before the doorway to the attic, he did not even see Minette waiting on the stair above him. *Dawn!* he thought as he noticed the grayness of the light.

But as he set foot on the last stair—as he had so many times before at dawn, on his way to take Clair-de-Lune to Brother Inchmahome—once again a paw came down in front of him.

The Monastery Is Hidden

When Clair-de-Lune emerged from the attic a half an hour later, she saw a strange thing.

It was Mrs. Costello's Minette, crouched on a stair with something in her mouth. A gray mouse tail dangled over her dainty black chin—and alongside it, glinting softly, a silver chain.

Clair-de-Lune froze. She had not been surprised that Bonaventure had not come to fetch her: she had thought he was working on his ballet. And she had been thinking, as she got up, about last night; she had been thinking about what she had heard when she had finally listened. She had been trying to understand it, for it still made no sense to her. And she had also been thinking, *How strange I feel this morning: light-headed and weak and warm all over.* But when she saw the cat, she felt a deep chill descend from the top of her head right down through her body.

Minette was staring at her with an odd, almost guilty expression on her face. Clair-de-Lune stamped her foot suddenly, and hissed. The cat dropped her burden, turned tail, and fled. And there on the stair, mortally wounded, was Bonaventure.

Clair-de-Lune covered her face with her hands. *No,* she wanted to say. *No. I will not let this be true. I will not.* But when she looked again she saw his tail twitch, and she ran down the stairs and threw herself down on the step beside him, peering down at his tiny body and hoping . . . hoping . . .

Feeling somebody near him, Bonaventure opened his eyes and said faintly, in a voice of deep affection:

"Ah . . . Mademoiselle Clair-de-Lune! How fortunate . . . that you have come by! For now I may say to you, *adieu!*—and God bless you!—and ask you to say the same to Brother Inchmahome. And perhaps you could tell him . . . ah, but he will understand."

Clair-de-Lune was crying so hard—and yet silently—that she could barely see him through her tears. And so she did not see the little silver thing he held even now in his paws, and which he was offering to her, insistently.

Dear Bonaventure, dear friend, she said brokenly, and she sounded not like a baby bird, but like a baby seal on the seashore keening for its mother. *You must not die! You must get well again! I will look after you! Brother Inchmahome and I will nurse you until you are well! And then we will protect you—we will keep you carefully—so that no cat—no cat—* Her tears fell on his fur, and she picked him up gently in her hands and held him against her breast and rocked as she held him.

"Ah!" said Bonaventure. "But, I ask myself, is that a life? The full life, dear mademoiselle, must have its Cats!" Then he stopped and gazed at her with a new expression on his face.

"And you see what has happened?" he added softly. "I can understand you! It is as Brother Inchmahome always said— only a matter of listening!

"But you are sad!" he continued very faintly, after what seemed like hours of silence, during which Clair-de-Lune held him and wept. "You must not be sad. For nothing can really go wrong in this house, you know. Not really. Not forever. No matter how bad it seems . . .

"And look!" he said, again holding up the locket. "Look what I have for you! It is . . . a gift! It is important. Promise me you will wear it! Promise me you will keep it—no matter what! And promise me you will show it to Brother Inchmahome!"

He was so insistent that Clair-de-Lune could do nothing but obey. So, carefully, and weeping all the while, she laid him in her lap. She took the locket from his paws and, with trembling fingers, fastened it round her neck. Then she picked him up again and cradled him against her breast.

"Good!" said Bonaventure in deep satisfaction. There was another long pause. Then:

"I can smell fish! I think . . . the Cat . . . left her fishy breath on me. . . . But fish . . . reminds me . . . of my home . . . by the sea. I think . . . I will return there. Farewell! Farewell!"

When Clair-de-Lune brought the dying mouse in her cupped hands up to her lips and kissed him, she felt his whiskery nose trembling against her skin one last time, in a mouse kiss. Then he spoke and danced and kissed no more.

Clair-de-Lune stayed weeping silently on the stair, the mouse cradled against her breast, for a long time. She did not think it true that nothing could go wrong. She thought something had gone desperately wrong, too wrong to be borne. When at last she had no more weeping left in her and grew still, she did not know what to do. She could no longer remember why she was out on the stairs.

Clair-de-Lune rose, and swayed where she stood. She leaned against the banister for support. She must get to the monastery. She must tell Brother Inchmahome. Only he would understand. Only he could make this unbearable thing bearable.

Clair-de-Lune began, with difficulty, to walk down the stairs. She passed one landing, then another. But where was the stone door? Uncertainly, she dragged herself down another flight. However, the next landing was Monsieur Dupoint's. She retreated hastily, went back up the stairs, passed one landing, then another, then another, until she almost stumbled upon the attic. Again, hastily, she retreated.

Where was the stone door? Where was it?

All at once fear gripped her. She must find it, she must . . . She began, unsteadily, to run, descending again to where she thought it must be. But it was not there! It was not there!

And now her head was spinning; she had to lie down. Perhaps if she lay down, things would seem clearer. She crept into the alcove under the stairway where she had found Bonaventure, curled up in the shadow with the mouse cradled against her chest, and—shivering, worrying, and quite hidden from passersby—fell into a feverish sleep.

๑ ๑ ๑

When Clair-de-Lune awoke many hours later, she could not even remember what had happened, was not even sure what she was holding cupped in her hands.

All she knew was that it was precious.

I must get home, she thought.

And so, step by step, she began scaling the twelfth flight of stairs, muttering to herself in the voice of a baby bird. Every stair seemed made of rock; surely she was climbing a mountain. Was that not sky above her, a waterfall to her right? But no, here was the door to the attic. She knocked as if she were a stranger.

Monsieur Dupoint answered the door.

"Ah, here she is, the little one. Thank God! But she is ill! Make haste, madame! We must get her to bed!"

And Clair-de-Lune felt herself being carried and then laid down on a bed.

"The child is burning up!" she heard Monsieur Dupoint say. "And what is this in her hand? A dead mouse? How strange!" He took the little body from Clair-de-Lune's limp hand and tossed it into the rubbish. "She must have a doctor," he continued, "and plain, wholesome food fit for an invalid—though she may not eat for some days. . . . So in the meanwhile, she must have barley water to drink: the best to be had! And you must keep her warm, madame. . . ."

But Clair-de-Lune's grandmother was sitting, inert, in a chair by the bed. Her stern, beautiful face was pale with shock. She swallowed, licked her lips, and spoke:

"We are too poor . . . ," she began, and trailed off. "There are things I can sell. . . ."

"Madame!" said Monsieur Dupoint, shaking his head and unconsciously holding out his hands, palms forward, in the position that is called *donner le coeur*, "to give the heart." "Do not distress yourself on this account. It is nothing. I will get the doctor and the barley water immediately. And I will arrange to have food sent up, for one never knows when she might feel equal to some nourishment . . . hopefully sooner rather than later! Then I will go to see the Company—and madame, if you don't mind my saying, surely you should have done so sooner. You are not receiving enough to live on, that is plain. I know they will be generous when I explain the circumstances. Everyone remembers your daughter with such affection. And everyone has such hopes for Clair-de-Lune!"

With that he hurried from the room.

When he was gone, Clair-de-Lune's grandmother undressed Clair-de-Lune, sponged her down carefully, and dressed her again in her nightgown. She saw the locket, but it was not familiar to her, and rather than fiddling with the clasp she left it be. She gave the child—who was tossing and turning and making strange little noises in her throat—a little water to drink, during which procedure Clair-de-Lune stared at her with wide, unseeing eyes.

Then she sat by the bed, staring into space, praying for the return of the silver-feathered bird with the red-gold heart.

Late, late that night, if anyone in the building had been up and out on the stairs, they would have seen a strange procession: four and twenty dancer mice making their way slowly up flight after flight of stairs.

When they reached the attic, they continued, one by one,

under the door and into Clair-de-Lune's home, where Clair-de-Lune lay tossing and turning with fever and her grandmother sat staring into the darkness, which was lit by a single candle flame.

Three of them scaled the sides of the small wicker wastepaper basket and with some difficulty managed to drag out the little body they found there. Then six of the mice lifted Bonaventure onto their shoulders, and the procession continued back out through the door and down the stairs.

All that night, there was the sound of mouse weeping all over the building. But it was so faint that only mice could hear it.

The Golden Cage

Not half an hour after Monsieur Dupoint hurried away, the doctor arrived, panting and puffing, at the top of the stairs. When he examined Clair-de-Lune, he looked grave.

"She is so thin, madame!" he said to Clair-de-Lune's grandmother. "If I did not know that she had a grandmother to look after her—that is, your good self—I would guess that she was starving! As it is, of course, that is scarcely possible. Nonetheless, a fever like this—well, a normal child would come through it. But she has so few reserves to call on. If she is ill for any length of time . . ." However, he shrugged, as if to signify that, after all, one never knew. Then he left a list of instructions and said he would call back in the morning.

Soon after the doctor left, the deliveries began to arrive, on the backs and in the arms of panting and puffing delivery boys who wore aprons over their shirtsleeves and trousers and who had to sit down for five minutes at the top of the stairs to recover. There were fruit and vegetables; there were jellies and junkets; there were two whole cases of lemon barley water, and even a bunch of fresh violets for the bedside table (Monsieur Dupoint had seen Clair-de-Lune in her best dress and indeed remembered her mother in it), which filled the attic with their scent.

But Clair-de-Lune knew none of this. Or at least, she knew none of it but the traipsing up and traipsing down the twelve flights of stairs, and it seemed to her that that was what she was doing, hour after hour, day after day, up the stairs, down the stairs. Only there were not twelve flights of them; instead they were never-ending, and all she knew was that she was holding something in her hand that was infinitely precious and looking for something that she could not find.

And all the while she wept and wept for Bonaventure, although she no longer remembered who he was.

Every day the doctor called, and every day he looked graver.

"She seems troubled about something," he muttered to himself. "And it is often matters of the heart and not the health that decide whether someone will live or die. . . ."

Then one night, he looked at Clair-de-Lune and only shook his head.

Clair-de-Lune had stopped tossing and turning; now she lay calmly and very still, breathing softly, with an expression on her face of great sadness.

Monsieur Dupoint was weeping. He had called every day to sit with Clair-de-Lune's grandmother, and to bring fresh flowers. But Clair-de-Lune's grandmother did not weep.

When the doctor left, she turned to Monsieur Dupoint and said steadily:

"Monsieur Dupoint, I wonder if you would be so kind as to sit with Clair-de-Lune for a little while. I must go out."

Poor lady, thought Monsieur Dupoint through his tears. "Of course, madame," he said. "You must have a walk, and breathe some fresh air. But pray, do not overstrain yourself. You, too, are frail."

Clair-de-Lune's grandmother put on her bonnet and *pelisse*—neither of which was accustomed to much use—and picked up a large brown paper package she had ready by the door. Then, quietly, she slipped out. Monsieur Dupoint, lost in his thoughts, did not even see her go.

Clair-de-Lune's grandmother may have seemed calm, but in fact she was half mad with grief and fear. Only someone half mad with grief and fear would go looking for a person she had not seen for twelve years in the same place she had last seen her, and expect her still to be there.

But if Clair-de-Lune's grandmother was half mad, she was also half sane, and perhaps she knew that the rules for fortune-tellers are different from those for ordinary people. Or perhaps she realized that the woman would know she was coming to see her, and so arrange to be where she could find her.

Through wind and rain Clair-de-Lune's grandmother went, and the brown paper package she held against her chest reminded her so strongly of the baby she had been clinging to the last time she had come this awful way that it was difficult for her to remember which occasion this was. *Now or then? Then or now?* the wind seemed to mutter. The buildings with their narrow alleys made tunnels for the wind to rush through, and Clair-de-Lune's grandmother was almost blown over by the force of it every time she passed an alley. At last she came to the alley she must turn into, and walking directly into the wind was so difficult that for a moment she feared it would defeat her. Finally, thrusting her whole weight against it, she managed to get to the door she sought, a third of the way down. Leaning against it, she knocked loudly with the brass door knocker.

Almost immediately the door opened, and Clair-de-Lune's grandmother found herself once more in the heavy darkness she knew so well from her dreams (for it sometimes seemed to her that she dreamed of it every night), the heavy darkness lit by the fire and the candles and scented by a perfume she did not recognize.

She laid her package on the table. The woman opened it and examined the dress she found inside, an evening dress of black velvet, La Lune's finest.

"This is my fee?" she said.

"I have no cash," said Clair-de-Lune's grandmother.

"It is more than I require," said the woman.

"No matter," said Clair-de-Lune's grandmother. "The child is dying." Suddenly she covered her face with her hands. "The doctor said she was starving. . . ."

"I tried to tell you!" said the woman. She was angry. It was as if their last conversation had taken place only a matter of minutes ago. "I tried to tell you that she could not have one without the other! That if she tried to do either one on its own, she would starve!"

"But all that is too late now! It is done! I have come to ask you, is there any hope? Can I undo what I have done? For I did it—you know I did it—to keep her safe from harm! It seems to me that fate is too cruel if what I did to keep her from harm—"

"Kills her?" said the woman. "I see what you mean. Well, it is simple. You must set the bird free."

Clair-de-Lune's grandmother wailed aloud. "But the bird is lost! It escaped years ago, when the child was still an infant."

"So much the better, then. Now it is up to the bird. But tell me, madame . . ." She leaned across the table and gazed into her client's eyes. "Do you still have the cage?"

Clair-de-Lune's grandmother hung her head.

"Then destroy it," said the woman briskly. "You must forswear any intention of ever caging the bird again. Then—well, perhaps the bird will return. I have told you all I know."

Clair-de-Lune's grandmother stumbled home through the wind and the rain. She was indeed frail, and as thin as Clair-de-Lune, and it was hard going. When at last she reached the attic—and it had taken her half an hour to climb the stairs—she would not have been surprised to find Clair-de-Lune still and cold. But no, the child was alive, breathing softly as she slept.

Poor Monsieur Dupoint slept also, having dropped off in his chair as he watched over her.

Clair-de-Lune's grandmother shook him softly by the shoulder, with a hand that was as thin as a claw.

"Madame!" he said, starting up. Then he added with concern, "Are you quite well?"

"Quite well, Monsieur Dupoint," she said steadily. "Thank you for your assistance. I will sit with her now."

When Monsieur Dupoint had gravely taken his leave, she stood for a moment by the bed, watching over Clair-de-Lune. Then she went to the trunk where she kept her daughter's clothes, and pulled something out of it. It was the golden cage in which the silver-feathered bird with the red-gold heart had once been confined. She built up the fire and threw the cage onto it. Then, drawing her chair close, she sat watching as it melted down steadily into a lump of metal, dully gold.

Only then, exhausted, did she creep to her bed and fall into a deep, untroubled sleep, for she knew she had done all she could.

The Lady

Late that night, as Clair-de-Lune lay breathing softly in her bed, she felt a tiny, whiskery nose trembling against her cheek.

Slowly—for she was very weak—she opened her eyes and turned her head on the pillow.

Bonaventure! she said, but she had not even the strength for the voice of a baby bird.

"You must accompany me immediately, mademoiselle!" said Bonaventure. "For a Lady awaits! She has requested an audience with you—and she has sent *me* to fetch you!"

A Lady! said Clair-de-Lune, in a voice so quiet that only a mouse could have heard it. *But Bonaventure, I fear I have not the strength to travel. . . .*

"Ah, mademoiselle!" said Bonaventure. "Feel, if you will, my shoulders!"

Clair-de-Lune was too weak to move her hand up to the pillow. But Bonaventure scampered down the bed to where it rested by her side, and placed himself underneath it. Feeling his warm fur against her fingers, she very softly stroked his back. Sure enough, she felt something there that she had never felt before. What were they, these fine feathery folded things?

"Wings!" said Bonaventure. "Now, if you will be so gracious as to arise from your couch, mademoiselle," he said importantly, "I shall support you!"

Even with wings, Clair-de-Lune doubted Bonaventure's ability to support a human child. But then, she knew, he had never held with Limitations of any kind.

Very slowly, she began to sit up. Just then a strange thing happened. She felt a force behind her, as strong as two strong arms, helping her up and out of bed. Suddenly she found herself standing, with a curious, weightless sensation in her arms and legs, as if all the weight was being taken by someone else. Bonaventure held her arm with his forepaws, his wings fluttering as swiftly as a honeyeater's.

"You see?" he said proudly. "And now we must set out! Look up!"

Clair-de-Lune looked up at the ceiling and found, to her surprise, that she was gazing at the starry night sky, as if suddenly the roof of the building had disappeared or become invisible. *Just like my dream!* she thought.

"The Lady," said Bonaventure solemnly, "dwells in the Land Behind the Stars."

But how will we get there? thought Clair-de-Lune. Just as she thought this, however, she noticed something in the sky above them, something that was not a star, a small something growing larger, descending lightly and yet surely toward them at extraordinary speed. All at once, before Clair-de-Lune had time to jump back—even if she had had the strength and co-ordination to do so—this thing fell, unwinding, into the attic from the sky, hitting the floor directly before her feet with a soft slap. She saw before her a rope ladder, made out of a substance that was white and silver and faintly glowing, as fragile as a spider's web and yet glinting like steel with strength.

"There is no place one needs to go to which there is no stairway—or ladder," remarked Bonaventure. "Let us away, mademoiselle!"

And so, supported from behind by the strength of a mouse with wings like a hummingbird's, Clair-de-Lune began to climb the rope ladder, up, up, up, step by step, handhold by handhold, into the black starry sky.

The ladder swayed slightly with her weight, but it was a gentle swaying, like a mother rocking from side to side as she holds her sleeping baby. As she climbed, Clair-de-Lune looked not only up and around her, but also below her (for she was completely unafraid), and the higher she went, the more she could see.

At first when she looked down, she saw only the attic—but of course she saw it from above, and she had never seen it like that before. And so she saw her own bed and the wooden floor and the big chest and the cupboard and even her sleeping grandmother, all from a distance. It was not long before her grandmother looked as small as a child.

But as she climbed higher, the attic seemed dwarfed among the vast expanse of red roofs so tightly built upon one another, which was the city in which Clair-de-Lune lived. No wonder she could see so little of the sky from down there! Dangling above, she could barely make out any break in the roofs at all.

As she climbed higher still, she discovered something that took her breath away. The city was a large, jagged circle, substantial even from a distance. But it did not go on forever. Outside the city, she saw now, were open fields on which the stars shone, and running through these fields were streams of fresh water, glinting and darting like giant eels, and beyond that, beyond the fields, the vast, silver expanse of the sea.

Already the city seemed small, so small that she felt tender toward it.

As Clair-de-Lune climbed higher and higher, she saw not only the sea, but other countries, other seas, places of ice and mountains and deserts; and finally she saw the whole world, a blue ball dropping farther and farther below her.

Soon the earth was so small that she felt tender toward it, too.

Then there came a dazing and a dazzling as she climbed and climbed, on and on, through a symphony of starlight above, around, and below her.

Finally, she paused on the gently swaying ladder to rest. And now another strange thing happened. For as she gazed around her, filled with wonder, it seemed to her that once again she was on a stage, staring out into a vast black cavern that was all the night sky, lit from above by a spotlight that was the moon.

Bonaventure's whiskers were tickling her ear.

"Look up!" he said again. "Look up, mademoiselle!"

Clair-de-Lune obeyed, and found herself gazing into the face of the moon.

Only it wasn't the moon. It was the pale oval face of a

woman, with a black night sky full of wild hair, and eyes like stars.

"The Lady!" whispered Bonaventure.

Clair-de-Lune gazed into the woman's face. The woman gazed back into Clair-de-Lune's.

And all at once Clair-de-Lune forgot the ladder, forgot her vast height. She let go and reached toward the Lady with all her strength, almost leaping upward in the effort, and in the split second before she felt herself beginning to fall she saw the woman's eyes widen in alarm and something else, a kind of pain. But then Bonaventure in his great new strength was behind her, pulling her back, and again her fingers curled reluctantly around the rope.

But it is my mother! she said, beside herself.

Yes, said the Lady, *I am your mother—*

"Nevertheless, if you please, mademoiselle," said Bonaventure earnestly into her ear, "do not, under any circumstances, let go of the ladder."

So Clair-de-Lune was still, and as the ladder swayed gently back and forth, she yearned and yearned toward the Lady, but only in her heart.

You left me! she said.

Ah! Against my will! said the Lady. *If you only knew!*

I do know. I do, said Clair-de-Lune. *The swan died, but she wanted to live.*

If you only knew how much! said the Lady. *But my heart was broken. . . .*

So was his! said Clair-de-Lune.

And I never said it, said the Lady. *I died trying to say it.*

May I not stay with you now? pleaded Clair-de-Lune.

The Lady gazed down at her, her eyes sparkling like stars with tears.

If you do, she said, *he will never know. And his heart will never heal.*

I love him! said Clair-de-Lune.

As do I! said the Lady. *But he does not know!*

They gazed at one another in silence, and Clair-de-Lune felt that, though half her heart was sleeping mile after mile through the darkness below her on the slowly turning earth, half was up here among the stars with the Lady, and that wherever she stayed, it would be split apart.

Now we will all have broken hearts! she said.

Say to him what I did not, pleaded the Lady. *Not from my heart, but from yours. My life is over. Yours is just beginning. But you can redeem my life—make everything right, all the past, everything!—by living your life freely, as I did not live mine. There is, you see, this magic in life. And if you do this, then all will be well.*

Her voice seemed to echo, like a bell ringing across the night:

All . . . will . . . be well!

"The dawn approaches!" whispered Bonaventure.

Live, Clair-de-Lune, said the Lady. *Live.*

Clair-de-Lune knew that she would soon have to climb back down and away from the Lady forever. Still she stood swaying on the rope ladder, gazing up into the Lady's face. The Lady gazed back at her, her wild black hair seeming to undulate in the sky, and her eyes twinkling with love.

A long time passed: as long as a lifetime, or a dream.

Then at last, reluctantly, Clair-de-Lune began to climb.

She climbed down, down, down, all the while gazing upward into the Lady's face, and as she climbed she felt herself enveloped in light, a soft, silver, embracing light, so filled with tenderness that Clair-de-Lune could feel no pain, although she knew that each step took her farther and farther away and that on the other side of this light she would be waking again into the ordinary world. As she climbed, the blue ball of the earth grew larger and larger, the countries of the world—the deserts and mountains, the lands of ice and the vast blue seas—nearer and nearer, and the glinting rivers and the countryside around her city closer and closer till at last she was climbing down the rope ladder into the room in the enchanted building whence she had come. But she never took her eyes off the moon, not even when, with Bonaventure's help, she lay back down in her bed and rested her head—which was filled with stars—on the pillow.

"Good night, Mademoiselle Clair-de-Lune!" she heard Bonaventure say. *"Au revoir!"*

Goodbye, my daughter, said the Lady's voice in her head. *Godspeed!*

And Clair-de-Lune lay once again in her bed, deeply asleep as the dawn of a new day spread over the sky, the locket that had been Bonaventure's last gift nestling in the little hollow of her throat.

Everything—and One Thing

Clair-de-Lune opened her eyes.

She was lying in her bed in the attic. It was morning, and very quiet. In the bed on the opposite side of the room, her grandmother lay sleeping: she knew by the sound of the old lady's breathing, although Clair-de-Lune felt too weak to move her head.

Then she realized that someone was holding her hand, and with a tremendous effort she turned her head very slightly to see who it was.

"Good morning," said Brother Inchmahome. He was sitting in a chair by the bed, looking down at her, his eyes as clear and gray as the dawn sky.

Clair-de-Lune smiled slowly.

"So," said Brother Inchmahome softly, "you have returned from your journey. I was very much afraid that you had decided to stay."

Very slightly, Clair-de-Lune shook her head. But then her eyes filled with tears.

"Bonaventure," said Brother Inchmahome. "I know. He loved and lost, you see! Ah, but did he lose, I wonder?"

Faintly but firmly, Clair-de-Lune shook her head.

There was a little pause. Brother Inchmahome got up and poured some barley water into a glass. Then he supported her head as she drank it. He laid her back down on the pillow and replaced the glass. Then he sat, holding her hand and listening, and Clair-de-Lune felt that he would have been quite content to stay there beside her forever. She gazed up into his face, and the tears fell steadily from her eyes, down her cheeks and into her hair, which was spread out around her on the pillow like a halo.

"And have you been neglecting your lessons while you have been away, so far from us?" said Brother Inchmahome softly.

Again Clair-de-Lune shook her head.

"Ah!" said Brother Inchmahome. "I thought not. You have returned from your long journey with an answer, it seems! Well, my dear," he added very gently, "we have days and days to speak of this. We need not speak of it now. Perhaps when you are stronger . . ."

But Clair-de-Lune shook her head, a little more firmly. The barley water was giving her strength.

"You want to speak of it now?"

Clair-de-Lune nodded.

Brother Inchmahome considered a moment. Then he said slowly, almost to himself, "Perhaps you need to speak of it—in order to start getting well . . ."

Clair-de-Lune nodded quite definitely. Brother Inchmahome almost laughed.

"Well, then!" he said, and leaned a little closer. "Do you remember what it was—the new question?" he asked gently.

Clair-de-Lune nodded.

But Brother Inchmahome sat silently for a moment, almost as if he was too moved to speak. And it seemed to Clair-de-Lune that the air around her at that moment had never been so quiet. Finally, he said—ah, with such tenderness!—"What is it, then, Clair-de-Lune? What is it that you want to say?"

Clair-de-Lune smiled slightly. Carefully, with as much effort as she could afford, she lifted her arms and described with her outstretched fingers the widest circle she could make.

Everything!

Then she lifted one index finger.

And one thing.

Brother Inchmahome smiled and bowed his head, to show that he understood. Then he said:

"And what is that one thing?"

Clair-de-Lune opened her mouth to say it, for she knew now that if she wanted to, she could speak. But just as the words were about to escape into sound, just as she was about to speak with her lips and her tongue and her voice for the first time, she understood: she understood!

For after all, what she wanted to say most of all could not be said in words.

And so instead she held out her arms, and Brother Inchmahome lifted her up in his own, and she hugged him with all the little strength that she had, for she knew that this said *I love you* better than words.

Just then, they both heard a sound—a beating, a breeze, the soft sound of something fluttering against the window above Clair-de-Lune's bed. They both looked across, and Brother Inchmahome, who was carrying Clair-de-Lune in his arms, frowned with wonder and amazement.

For it seemed to him that he saw a silver-feathered bird, whose red-gold heart glowed like a flame through its breast, beating its wings against the windowpane, as if it wanted to get in.

What could he do but obey it?

Kneeling on Clair-de-Lune's bed, he leaned over and opened the casement. Immediately the bird flew into the room, across Clair-de-Lune's bed, and into her heart.

And Clair-de-Lune looked into Brother Inchmahome's eyes, as gray as water flowing over stone, as gray as a dawn sky—as gray as her own—and said, in a voice that had never been heard in all the world in all of time before:

"Your eyes always seem to be looking at beautiful things."

And Brother Inchmahome said:

"I always am."

Then his eyes fell on the locket, which was resting just above her nightgown in the little hollow of her throat, and all at once the color drained from his face.

"Where did you get this?" he whispered.

For the hinge had come open, and there before him was a picture of a young man, not much more than a boy. He had long black curly hair, this lad; he had a kind, heart-shaped face with an exceptionally high forehead; he had clear gray eyes; and though he was clean-shaven, the stubble of his dark beard peppered the lower half of his face with an infinite number of tiny black dots.

The boy had a remarkable expression on his face, as if he was looking at the most beautiful thing in the world.

Brother Inchmahome's mind was whirling, whirling into the past.

It was a picture of his younger self.

The Disreputable Young Man

"Please," said the young man. His voice was hoarse with desperation, his long dark hair soaked with rain, his eyes burning in his gaunt face. "I have nothing to give you. But it would mean everything to me. We were engaged to be married."

He was standing huddled at the stage door in the wind and the rain; he was pleading with the burly doorman, who stood solidly, his arms folded, in the doorway.

The doorman pricked up his ears at that.

"Engaged?" he said, looking him up and down. "So—it was you, eh? Well, I'll tell you one thing, mate. It'd cost me more than my life is worth to let you in. Go on, now. Off you go! And if you take my advice, you'll keep right away. . . ." But then he took pity on the thin young man, whose wild, helpless misery was only too apparent. "Here," he said, reaching into his pocket. "Buy yourself a meal. And forget her, mate. These dancers—here today, gone tomorrow. They ain't substantial. Don't even eat enough to keep 'emselves alive. What you need's a nice bonny round girl like my Elsie. . . ."

But the young man had drifted off, zigzagging first this way, then that, like one who had been hit.

"Watch the traffic," called the doorman as a hansom cab swerved to avoid him. But the young man stumbled on, oblivious.

"What a night!" muttered the doorman to himself. "What with Mademoiselle Moon 'erself givin' up the ghost all of a sudden and the weather like it is! It's enough to engender truly morbid thoughts in a man, s'welp me!" He hunched his shoulders and drew his coat more tightly about him as the sound of weeping drifted down the stairs behind him.

"They wouldn't let her see me," said Brother Inchmahome as the tears streamed down his face. He had set Clair-de-Lune down gently, almost absently, on the bed and sat beside her, talking quickly, his voice breaking like a boy's. "It was so sudden! We were in love! We had been seeing each other every day, whenever she could. But then one day—silence! I sent letters, but they came back unopened. I didn't know if it was her—or them."

He held his head in his hands.

"So I would go to the theater to see her dance," he began again after a moment, and in his voice there was more and more pain. "I knew she was unhappy, but I couldn't help her! I couldn't help her!

"I was there the night she died. And still they wouldn't let me see her, not even to say goodbye—forever. I had lodgings in this building. I came back here—through the wind and rain—when there was no more hope. I wanted to lie down and die. But I couldn't find the floor! I just kept climbing, climbing, climbing the stairs! It was like a kind of hell. Climbing the stairs, and knowing she was dead. And not being able to get home . . .

"I went up, I went down. I thought I'd gone mad. And then—then I found this new place, a floor I hadn't seen before, and a door . . . and a monastery. . . . They welcomed me, the brothers. They said I was waiting for something.

"I thought it was death! I thought it was death! I was so lonely! But I learned to listen—and the listening began to heal me."

Then he looked at Clair-de-Lune.

"But life," he whispered, "never ends—only begins, over and over again. . . ."

"She sewed it into her *tutu*, next to her heart," said Clair-de-Lune dreamily, as if telling a story that she was hearing for the first time. And as she told it she saw her mother sewing, awkwardly, as the tears streamed down her face, afraid every moment that Madame Nuit would catch her. "A picture of you!"

"She asked for one, just before she stopped seeing me."

"She was wearing it the night she died."

"And there was a child!" he whispered. "She—had—"

"She died trying to say something. Do you know what she was trying to say?"

"What was she trying to say?" said Brother Inchmahome as he stroked her face and hair.

"She was trying to say, 'I love you.' She must have known you were there. She must have thought you might hear. And

190

she knew you didn't know that she still did love you. She died," said Clair-de-Lune, "of a broken heart, because they wouldn't let her stay with you. And I lost my mother and my father. But now," she added softly, "all will be well, for I have found you."

Again she held out her arms, and he took her up and held her as if he would never let her go.

Not ten feet from where Clair-de-Lune and her father held each other, on and on, with all their strength, Clair-de-Lune's grandmother lay suspended between sleeping and waking.

It was morning. She must get up. There was work to be done, duties to perform. . . .

But still she lay, drifting, drifting, too tired, and somehow too happy, to rise.

She could hear Clair-de-Lune's voice, weak like a chick's, and yet filled, like a chick's, with the force of life, and knew that she would live, and that she could speak, and that the bird had returned after all.

Clair-de-Lune's grandmother breathed more and more quietly. No, her granddaughter would not die. She would be a great dancer—Madame Nuit saw the performances, and the notices, the flowers and the long curtain calls; all these passed like a pageant before her closed eyes. She would dance as no one, not even her mother, had danced before her.

She would not die. And there would be no disreputable young man, no broken heart. Clair-de-Lune's grandmother heard the soft voice of Brother Inchmahome and smiled. The child was safe. All was well.

Clair-de-Lune's grandmother felt herself drifting, drifting on a calm blue sea toward a beautiful island, her work done.

She had done her best. She had done her best. It was time . . . time . . .

To rest.

And in the soft morning light, the lump of metal, dully gold, in the cold fireplace—the lump of metal that had once been the cage—looked like nothing so much as a heart.

The Island of Day

In Bonaventure's mouse hole, three floors below, the four and twenty members of Bonaventure's company sat mourning together. Some held paws or leaned against one another, staring into space. Others wept quietly into tiny handkerchiefs.

For days they had met like this, not knowing what else to do.

As the news of Bonaventure's death had spread around the mouse community, mice—not only those connected with his school and company, but also many whose lives had touched his in more accidental ways, and even some who had never met him—had come, in ones and twos and threes, carrying spring flowers foraged from everywhere you might expect a fresh flower to have accidentally fallen, and little stumps of candles. Bit by bit, the mouse hole had filled up with them, the flowers and the little winking lights, and now it was a magical place, like an enchanted cave that might be the setting for the kind of ballet Bonaventure himself might have written.

But no one in his company had danced since the morning he died.

That terrible night, following mouse tradition, they had all journeyed solemnly up to the sixth floor to collect his poor noble body, while others—Leonard and Virginia, several mice from the Duke of Wellington, and the mouse who lived in the organ at St. Mary's among them—had built a special raft from twigs. They had laid him upon it, wept and prayed over him, and launched the raft into the underground stream beneath the street outside, which they knew led straight to the sea. Thus Bonaventure had begun his journey home.

And yet they all knew he was still with them.

Juliet dreamed of him every night.

Perhaps this was why, at last, Rudolph spoke.

He had been sitting in the corner, below the picture of Arabella Moncrief, holding Margot's paw and thinking deeply. Now he stood and looked round at them earnestly. For a moment he hesitated. Then:

"My fellow mice!" he began. "This is not what he would have wanted. I am sure of it! He would have said, 'The show must go on!' Would he not?"

They all looked up at him.

"You're right, my love," said Margot. She had exchanged her usual pink ribbon for a black one, to show respect. "I can hear him saying it."

Absently, Rudolph pushed his spectacles back up his nose.

"I had no interest in learning to dance," he continued humbly, "but Bonaventure enthused me, and now"—here he looked at Margot, who smiled tearfully back at him—"The Dance is my life."

"And mine," said Margot softly.

"Bonaventure was a true *artiste*—not because he was dedicated, hardworking, and visionary, although he was certainly all of these, but because he was inspired by Love. My fellow mice, art that is not inspired by Love—art that is fed merely by the hope of fame or glory, for example—is art that is not worthy of the name! Bonaventure loved The Dance, and he loved others—that is why he wanted to share it with them. For him, Love was the most important thing in the world. But he knew that dancing was important, too, because it is one way, among many, to love.

"We show our love for him by grieving. But we can also show our love for him by carrying on his work. He gave his love of The Dance to us. Now we must give it to others.

"I propose," Rudolph said, drawing himself up bravely, "I propose that we go ahead with the performance, as a memorial to, and celebration of, our much-loved teacher, the *maestro* Bonaventure."

They were all silent for a moment. Then, spontaneously, they burst into applause, their tiny paws tapping against one another like the pitter-patter of the lightest shower of rain. Rudolph nodded once or twice, acknowledging their appreciation, and then sat down again, trembling with emotion. Margot slipped her paw into his and gazed at him lovingly. She had never been so proud of anyone in all her life.

That strange little sound of mice clapping took quite some time to die away. When it did, there was a short pause.

"But," said the mouse from the Duke of Wellington finally, "not meaning to make difficulties, guv, and, might I say, appreciating your sentiments with all my 'eart—the thing is, even if we was to—even if we tried to—"

"We have no Mouse Prince!" said little Juliet simply. "And what is *The Prince's Quest* without our Prince?"

They all sighed, murmuring agreement. Some began to cry again.

But Rudolph would not give up.

"Well, then," he pursued, "as I'm sure the *maestro* would have said, we must find one, my friends. He will not, of course, be Bonaventure. But—well—he will be himself."

And just then there was a knock at the entrance.

They all looked up.

There was a strange mouse standing in the doorway. He was thin and weary and travel-worn. But his fur was like black silk, and the light of a beautiful soul shone in his eyes.

"Excuse me," he said, "but is this not the school of the famous Monsieur Bonaventure, the teacher of the newly developed mouse ballet?"

"It is," said Rudolph gently. "But—"

"Ah," said the mouse, stepping inside. "Then at last I have found you. I have traveled to the city with one dream—to become a mouse dancer! But of course I may prove unworthy, and so no contribution, however small, to your noble endeavor would be too humble for me! If you would allow me to assist you in any capacity, you would make me happier than I could ever tell you! For I intend to devote my life to the cause of mouse dancing."

He stood looking round at them, his black eyes shining. And his dark princely figure, silhouetted in the doorway, looked so noble and knightly, and the spirit that shone from him was so beautiful, that they all knew at once that a new star had risen, and that Bonaventure's great dream would come true after all.

Clair-de-Lune and Brother Inchmahome stood hand in hand on the threshold of the stone door. And all the world was before them! But the world was very big. So, for a moment, they hesitated.

"Where shall we go?" said Clair-de-Lune, looking up into Brother Inchmahome's face, rather as if the question had not occurred to her before this moment.

Brother Inchmahome was wearing a black frock coat over light gray trousers, a white shirt with the high collar of the day, an embroidered waistcoat, and a violet tie. None of it fitted very well, for it was all borrowed, but the hair on the crown of his head had grown back, and he looked young—almost, though not quite, as young as in the miniature in the locket. He looked kindly down at Clair-de-Lune, whose fair hair shone almost silver against her black mourning dress and bonnet, as he searched for an answer.

"I think," said Brother Inchmahome at last, "that it doesn't much matter where we go, as long as we're together."

"I agree," said Clair-de-Lune. And they stepped out into the world together.

For the dream was over; the day had begun. And the Island of Day in the Ocean of Dreams was fair as fair as fair.

Cassandra Golds was born in Sydney, Australia, and grew up reading Hans Christian Andersen, C. S. Lewis, and Nicholas Stuart Gray over and over again—and writing her own stories as soon as she could hold a pen. She wrote *Clair-de-Lune* after coming upon the fascinating fact that many people have difficulty saying their own name without "pulling back" their voice. When she was a little girl, she went to ballet lessons at a dancing school quite as intriguing as the one in this book. And she did some of her growing up in an old-fashioned apartment building almost as magical as Clair-de-Lune's.